Visit the author, Jim Denney, at
www.denneybooks.com/timebenders.html.

TIMEBENDERS

DOORWAY TO DOOM

JIM DENNEY

Tommy NELSON®

www.tommynelson.com

A Division of Thomas Nelson, Inc.
www.ThomasNelson.com

Text copyright © 2002 Jim Denney

Published in Nashville, Tennessee, by Tommy Nelson®, a Division of Thomas Nelson, Inc.

Library of Congress Cataloging-in-Publication Data

Denney, James D.
    Doorway to doom / by Jim Denney.
      p. cm. — (Timebenders ; #2)
    Summary: Max and several of his middle school friends go through the Doorway of the Ages back to the Middle Ages, where their faith helps them stand up to a cruel king and his evil alchemist.
    ISBN 1-4003-0040-1
    [1. Time travel—Fiction. 2. Middle Ages—Fiction. 3. Christian life—Fiction.] I. Title.

PZ7.D4272 Do 2002
[Fic.]—dc21   2002023890

Printed in the United States of America

02 03 04 05 06 PHX 5 4 3 2 1

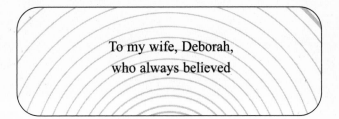

To my wife, Deborah,
who always believed

CONTENTS

1

THE DOOR OF A THOUSAND YEARS

It was long past midnight, and Max McCrane couldn't sleep.

It was the night before the big end-of-school party that Max and his friends Allie O'Dell and Grady Stubblefield had been planning for weeks—it was going to be the biggest party in the history of Victor Appleton Middle School. Max's mind was abuzz with plans for the big event.

Then he heard the footsteps downstairs.

Max sat up and listened. It wasn't unusual for Max to hear his father, who was an inventor, puttering around downstairs after midnight working on one of his projects or reading in his study.

The best thing to do when you can't sleep, he thought, *is raid the refrigerator. I could really go for a cold meat loaf-and-ketchup sandwich—and maybe Dad'll want one, too.* Max put on his slippers and his glasses, slipped quietly out of his bedroom, and crept down the stairs. Reaching the entryway at the bottom of the stairs, Max stopped and listened.

Across the entryway was his father's study. It was a big wood-paneled room, lined from floor to ceiling with books, and filled with antiques. Max walked to the study and pushed the door open. The hinges groaned. "Dad," he whispered, "would you—"

Max stopped. His eyes snapped wide open.

There was a man in the study—but he was *not* Max's father. He was over six feet tall and dressed in a hooded purple cloak over flowing robes of velvety black. He was old and had a long, gray beard; bushy, gray eyebrows; and dark, stormy eyes.

The man had been rummaging through the books on the shelves. A dozen books were scattered on the carpet. The stranger held a book in his hands and he looked up from it, directly into Max's eyes.

The strange man pointed a long, bony finger at Max. "Come here, lad!" he said in a voice like a creaking door.

For a moment, Max was frozen in place. Then he slammed the door shut, turned the key, and pulled it out of the lock. The intruder was trapped in the study.

"Dad! Mom!" Max yelled, running to the foot of the staircase. Behind him, the door of the study shook and rattled. Max's heart fluttered like bat wings. "Dad! Mom!" he shouted again. "There's a burglar in the study!"

"Coming, Max!" his dad called out. Though it seemed to Max like an eternity, it was only seconds later that Max's dad came running and stumbling down the stairs in his pajamas, his hair wild, his thick-lensed glasses askew on his nose. Max's mother came a few steps behind, face pale with fear, pulling her robe on as she ran down the stairs.

Max's father reached the bottom of the stairs. "What's wrong?"

"The burglar's in there, Dad!" Max shouted, pointing to the study. "I locked him in!"

"Oh, my!" Mrs. McCrane turned to her husband. "Oswald, I'll call nine-one-one!"

"Wait, dear," Dr. McCrane said. "I'll handle this." He turned to Max. "Are you *sure* you saw a burglar, Max? You didn't just have a bad dream?"

"I really saw the guy, Dad," Max said firmly. His breathing made a wheezing sound.

"I'll get your asthma inhaler, Max," Mrs. McCrane said. She went away, leaving Max and Dr. McCrane standing in the entryway.

"Wait here, Max," Dr. McCrane said. Max's father dashed into the living room and returned with a fireplace poker. He turned to Max. "On the count of three, open the door." He raised the poker. "Ready, Max?"

"Ready, Dad," Max said. He put the key into the lock and prepared to turn it. His hand shook.

Dr. McCrane set his jaw. "One . . . two . . . *three!*"

Max turned the key, grasped the knob, and pushed the door open. Dr. McCrane rushed into the study. Max expected to hear shouts, threats, the sound of a struggle. Instead, he heard . . . Nothing.

Max peered around the door and saw his father in the middle of the study, the fireplace poker hanging limply at his side. The strange old man in the hooded cloak was gone.

Max walked into the study and nervously looked all around. He carefully peeked behind his dad's favorite over-stuffed leather chair and ottoman—no one there. Nor could anyone be hiding behind the antique globe, the carved mahogany umbrella stand, or the flimsy-looking William IV armchairs. The stranger seemed to have simply—*vanished.*

"That's impossible!" Max said. "He was here, honest! He looked like some old wizard!"

Max's father put his finger to his lips, as if to say, *Shhh!* He pointed toward the elaborate Doorway at the far end of the room.

The Doorway was the oldest of all the antiques in the old McCrane House. Max's grandfather had found it in a London antique shop after the end of World War II. It had been salvaged from a crumbling old castle in the north of England. It was so ornate and richly decorated that Max imagined it had once adorned the entrance to a king's throne room or treasury room. Now, however, it was just the door of his father's closet.

The door itself was made of oak with inlaid panels,

warped and stained with age. The doorframe consisted of a pair of richly carved doorposts, topped by an elaborately carved lintel. The lintel and doorposts were covered in a thin layer of gold. Set into the pillars and lintel were crystals of clear quartz. Each crystal was about an inch in diameter, cut with facets like huge diamonds. There were twenty-seven crystals in all—ten spaced along each doorpost and seven spaced across the lintel. Jutting out of the doorframe on the right-hand side was a cup-shaped receptacle of blackened metal that, a thousand years earlier, was probably shiny brass.

Dr. McCrane gripped the fireplace poker and motioned Max to stand away from the Doorway.

Just then, Mrs. McCrane returned with Max's inhaler. "Oh, Oswald!" she said in a shrill voice, clutching her robe. "Please be careful!"

Max and his dad turned and gave her a *Shhh!* sign with their fingers to their lips. Then Dr. McCrane grasped the iron door handle and pulled. The door swung on rasping iron hinges. Dr. McCrane raised the poker—

But no one was there. The closet was empty except for some cardboard boxes and cobwebs.

"Well, Max," Dr. McCrane said, "it looks like your strange old man either vanished—or he never existed in the first place."

"Look, Dad," Max said, pointing to the floor. A dozen or so books were scattered on the Persian rug.

"Hmm," Dr. McCrane said. "How did those books get on the floor?"

"The burglar did it, Dad," Max said. "When I opened the door, he was standing right there, with one of your books in his hands."

"Oh, Oswald," Mrs. McCrane said, putting one hand to her mouth.

"I tell you, Dad, he was really here," Max insisted.

"Max, let's approach this scientifically," Dr. McCrane said, kneeling to pick up the books. "You know people do not simply disappear from locked rooms. So, logically, this burglar never existed—or he'd be in this room right now."

"I know what I saw, Dad," Max said. "The guy talked to me! When I locked him in, he pounded on the door!"

But Dr. McCrane didn't seem to be listening. He had put the books back on the shelf in alphabetical order—and there was a gap where a book should have been. "That's odd," he said. "One book is missing—Thaxter Butterworth's *Rockets and Modern Warfare*."

"Was it a thick book with a dark blue cover, and yellow lettering on the front?" Max asked.

"Why, yes," Dr. McCrane said, blinking behind his thick glasses. "How did you know?"

"Because," Max said, "that's the book the old guy was looking at when I opened the door. He must have taken it."

"But that's impossible," Dr. McCrane said—though he

didn't sound so sure anymore. "Let's leave. I want to lock up this room."

"Oswald," Mrs. McCrane said, "shouldn't we call the police?"

Dr. McCrane thought it over. "No," he said at last. "After all, what can we tell them? An old man in a wizard costume came into our house, stole a book, then vanished from a locked room? Who would believe a crazy story like that?" He shook his head and sighed. "Let's try to get some sleep. Maybe this will all make sense in the morning."

But as Max and his parents went back up the stairs, none of them really thought it would.

A thousand years earlier . . .

High in a castle tower, an old man in dark robes stepped through a golden Doorway from the future. The sound of his heavy boots echoed in the stone-walled chamber. The darkened room was lit only by two torches in iron brackets on the walls. The windows were shuttered.

The chamber was filled with scientific equipment, but the "science" practiced here was of that dark and primitive kind called *alchemy*. More superstition than science, alchemy was a search for such things as a potion that would enable people to live forever, or the secret for turning cheap lead into costly gold. The old alchemist did not think of himself as a wizard, though he looked like one. He thought of himself as a man of science.

The old man closed the door of the Doorway. He was angry with himself. A boy from the future had caught him and locked him in the room. He felt like a fool for being surprised that way—but at least he had proved that the Doorway worked. By his calculations, it had transported him about a thousand years into the future. Unfortunately, he had only gotten to spend about five minutes in that future, and all of it in just one room—some sort of library or study, from the looks of it. But if the Doorway had worked once, it would work again.

He threw back the hood of his purple satin cloak, revealing a face lined with age; a balding head fringed with long, gray hair; a hawk nose; and long, gray beard. In his bony fingers, he clutched a book with a dark blue cover and yellow lettering that read:

Rockets and Modern Warfare
by
Thaxter O. Butterworth

He placed the book on a heavy oak laboratory table. The table was arranged with beakers, flasks, amphoras, gallipots, retorts, alembics, a crucible, a mortar and pestle, and other objects used in experiments by alchemists of the Middle Ages—that dark and superstitious period from A.D. 500 to 1500.

The old man turned to the Doorway. It was, of course, the same Doorway that would stand a thousand years later in the home of Max McCrane—but now it was shiny and brand-new. The hinges were bright and polished. Its twenty-seven quartz crystals shone with a liquid light.

The Doorway didn't lead to another room. It simply stood near one end of the room, its threshold fastened to the floor, its lintel fastened to one of the bare wooden rafters of the ceiling.

There was a shiny brass receptacle in one doorpost. The old man reached into the receptacle and removed a glowing stone. Instantly, the glowing quartz crystals in the doorframe went dark. The stone in his hand gleamed with a pale yellow-green light; he called it a *moonstone*. He carefully placed it in a clear glass beaker on the lab table.

He opened a window shutter, and the chamber was instantly flooded with sunlight. He set the glass beaker with the moonstone on the window sill. Bending close to it, he spoke to the moonstone.

"Bathe in the sunlight, little stone. Tomorrow, you'll send me across the centuries once more—" His eyes clouded. "And if I see that meddlesome lad again, he'll be sorry he interfered!"

2

THE PARTY ON
THE EDGE OF FOREVER

The music was too loud. The lights and decorations were totally over-the-top. And there was *way* too much food.

The party was *perfect*.

The trees at the edge of the yard were strung with thousands of tiny blue lights. Hidden among the trees were fog machines, spewing cool clouds of mist upon the warm June evening. Multicolored lasers and spotlights shone on a revolving mirror ball suspended on wires over the grassy square. A strobe fired high-intensity light to the beat of the music.

It had been a strange day for Max. Despite all the activity of last-minute preparations, his mind had continually returned to the mystery of the previous night. Max prided himself on his rational, scientific mind—but a strange old character who disappeared from a locked room in the middle of the night—well, that just wasn't rational. It was downright *weird*.

Only when the party preparations were complete was he able to shake that feeling of strangeness. Once the guests began arriving, Max's thoughts finally turned away from the previous night's mystery.

It was Max's job to greet the guests at the garden gate and place a check mark by the name of each arrival on the guestlist. As the guests streamed through the gate, Max was relieved to see that one guest in particular had not yet shown up: Toby Brubaker.

Allie O'Dell stood behind the refreshment table, dressed in blue overalls and a white designer tee shirt. Her carrot-red hair was tied in a ponytail with a white scrunchie. She smiled, and multicolored party lights glinted off her braces.

The refreshment table was laden with steaming hot pizza, burritos, chicken nuggets, sausage rolls, fried mozzarella sticks, make-your-own tacos, onion rings, fried potato skins, and cheese-stuffed jalapeño poppers. Farther down the table were the cold foods—sub sandwiches, snack crackers, potato chips, tortilla chips, four kinds of dip, two kinds of salsa, guacamole, a bowl of candy bars (the little ones, marked "Fun Size!"), salted nuts, six colors of fruit punch, make-your-own banana splits, and a platter full of gross-looking green things.

Noah Claypool was first through the food line. He was short, dark-haired, and as skinny as a necktie—and had the biggest appetite of any kid at Victor Appleton Middle School. His plate was heaped with nothing but pizza.

"Noah," Allie said, "you're only having pizza?"

"Why not?" Noah replied. "Pizza is nature's perfect food!" He held up a slice, dripping pepperoni grease on his shoes. "It covers all your basic nutritional groups. You've got your crust for your bread group, your tomato sauce for your veggie group, and your cheese for, like, calcium or whatever, and your pepperoni for your fatty food group."

"Well, what about your dessert group?" Allie asked.

"Dessert has its own group?" Noah asked.

"Sure!" Allie said. "Try one of these." She picked up the platter of gross-looking green things and offered it to him. The green things were about the size and shape of prunes, but the glistening green color reminded Noah of something even more disgusting than prunes.

"What are they?" he asked, wrinkling his nose.

"My own secret recipe," Allie said, flashing a crooked smile.

Noah shrugged uncertainly, then took one of the shiny green wads from the platter and popped it in his mouth. His eyes lit up. The green stuff tasted sweet and melted on his tongue. "Whoa!" he said. "What are these?"

Allie giggled. "They're called Allie O'Dell's Tasty Green Boogers."

"Well, give me more!" He took a handful and put them on his plate, next to the pizza pile. "Allie, your boogers are awesome!"

"Thanks, Noah," Allie laughed. "So's your earwax!"

Grady Stubblefield sat at a small table, using a laptop computer to operate the special effects system. Grady was an African-American boy with an athletic build, short-cropped hair, shining eyes, and a broad smile.

"Yo, Stubblefield," a voice behind him said. "Radical bash, dude." Grady turned and saw Tommy Chu approaching, a sub sandwich in his fist. Tommy was a skater and a party animal. If Tommy Chu called your party a "radical bash," that was high praise indeed.

Tommy leaned over Grady's shoulder, checking out the laptop screen. He noticed the screen icons labeled *Spotlights*, *Strobes*, *Lasers, Fog*, *Sound*, *Video1,* and *Video2*. "Cool!" Tommy said. "You operate everything from one laptop?"

"Yeah," Grady said. "Max's dad designed all this stuff and showed me how to use it. The computer uses radio frequency to control it all—lights, music, fog, video projectors, everything."

"Radical," Tommy said. Then he leaned closer to Grady's ear. "Hey, man, have you seen Brubaker around?"

Grady got a creepy feeling at the mention of Toby Brubaker's name. He and Max had been against inviting Toby, but Allie had insisted. She believed that if you just "reached out" to people, no matter how mean they were, they just *might* change. Well, Grady couldn't argue—his own life was proof that people *could* change.

"I haven't seen Toby," Grady said. "Maybe he's not coming."

"Oh, he'll be here," Tommy said. "I heard him talking at lunch yesterday, and he's got plans, man."

"Plans?" Grady asked. "What kind of plans?"

Tommy shrugged. "He didn't specify. All I know is he wants to trash this party. Remember what he did to Jodi Broccoli's bash last year?"

Grady got a sick feeling at the mention of Jodi's party. Someone had phoned ten pizza shops and ordered a bunch of pizzas from each one. A hundred pizzas had arrived at Jodi's front door. While Jodi's parents and guests were at the front door, *someone* mixed all the ice cream and soda pop together. It foamed all over the table and onto the floor, ruining the carpets. Jodi's dad had a screaming fit and threw everybody out of the house—and Jodi still hadn't recovered from the humiliation. Though it couldn't be proved, no one doubted that Toby Brubaker was the culprit.

"Toby has plans, huh?" Grady said. "Well, I'll watch for him."

"Good luck," Tommy said.

As Tommy Chu walked away, Grady scanned the crowd, but saw no sign of Toby.

"Ready for me to take over, Grady?" Max's dad asked as he came up behind Grady. "You can get something to eat."

"Cool," Grady said. He let Max's dad take his place at the computer. But Grady wasn't thinking about getting something to eat. He was thinking about Toby.

At the same moment, a thickset boy was sneaking through the walnut grove behind the McCranes' backyard. He had a butch haircut, a pale, doughy face, a pug nose, and beady green eyes. He wore khaki pants and a blue long-sleeved tee shirt with a designer logo on the back. His name was Toby Brubaker, and he carried a big paper bag.

The bag was full of nasty surprises.

Toby's idea of a good time was making sure other people had a bad time. The happiest moment of his life had been the time he made a shambles of Jodi Broccoli's party. But Toby planned to have even *more* fun tonight.

Like a spy on a secret mission, he paused in the inky shadows behind a huge old walnut tree. He scratched an itchy spot in the middle of his forehead, then peered out from behind the tree.

Just a short distance ahead was the refreshment table— and standing next to the table was Allie. Dude, if only she would—Whoa! Excellent! Mrs. McCrane was calling Allie away from the table. The refreshments were unguarded—now was his chance!

Toby crept forward, a skulking shadow among the trees.

Mrs. McCrane and Allie were only in the house for two minutes. They returned to the refreshment table with big platters of buffalo wings. Allie set hers down, then cleared a place for Mrs. McCrane's platter. "Thanks, Allie," Max's mom said, shouting over the music. "The food's all on the table. Go have a good time!"

"Well," Allie said, "if you're sure—"

"*Eeeuuw!* Sick!"

Allie and Mrs. McCrane turned. The cry of disgust came from Salina Chavez, who made a terrible face while spitting black and white chunks into a napkin.

Allie rushed around the table. "What's wrong, Salina?" she asked.

"Gross!" Salina said. "There's something wrong with these cookies!"

"What cookies?" Allie asked. "We're not serving cookies."

"Then what are those?" Salina asked. She pointed to a plate of chocolate cookies with white filling.

Allie picked up a cookie, pulled it apart, and sniffed the filling. "Yuck! Somebody scraped out the frosting and filled them with toothpaste! Salina, this is somebody's sick idea of a gag."

"Yeah," Salina said, grimacing, "and I'm the one who's gagging!"

"*Yow!* The pizza's staring at me!" yelled Noah Claypool.

Allie whirled and saw Noah near the pizza tray. He lifted the foil, and there, scattered among the pizza slices, were eyeballs—half a dozen of them. And the eyeballs not only stared, they *glowed*.

Allie picked up one of the eyeballs—and almost dropped it in disgust. It felt warm, slithery, and alive. It was a glow-in-the-dark eyeball, the kind you could buy in any toy store or novelty shop. Allie shoved the eyeball in the pocket of her overalls—

And then she spotted Toby! He was grinning at her, enjoying his little prank.

"I thought so!" Allie said. "A prank like this has Toby Brubaker written all over it!"

Toby turned and melted into the crowd.

Standing at the gate, greeting guests, Max felt relieved. The atmosphere, the music, the food, everything was perfect—and Toby had apparently decided not to show. It looked like the party would be a success.

"Hey, Max!"

Max turned and saw Grady approaching.

"Everything's going great, huh?" Max said.

Grady shrugged. "I think so. Did Toby show up?"

Max grinned. "No sign of him."

"Toby's here, all right," another voice said. Max and Grady turned and saw Allie approaching. "He's been messing with the refreshment table!"

"But how did he get in without—," Max began, and then he slapped his forehead. "Duh! He sneaked in the back way!"

"I *knew* we shouldn't have invited him!" said Grady.

"He *sneaked* in, Grady," Allie pointed out. "He could have done that, invited or not. We did the right thing in telling him he's welcome."

"Yeah," Grady said. "I guess you're right. We just have to find him before he does any more damage."

"Let's split up," Max said. "Allie, you go that way. Grady—"

"Oh, Max!" a silky voice behind him said.

Max turned and saw Luna Skyes and Paul Majarian coming through the archway. Luna's hair was ultrablond, somewhere between gold and platinum. She was dressed in a coral-pink outfit with coral-pink dangles and coral-pink lip gloss. To Max, the whole effect seemed a little too . . . pink.

Luna turned to her escort and said, "Paul, do me a teensy favor, hmm? Go get us a couple of plates—anything vegetarian. I'll meet you at the picnic tables, 'kay? Ta-ta!"

"Sure, Luna," Paul said. He was tall, dark, and his

Adam's apple bobbed up and down when he talked. His big puppy-dog eyes gazed adoringly at Luna. He hurried off toward the refreshments.

"Come on, Max," Allie said.

"Excuse me, Allie, dear," Luna said, wrapping her arm around Max's. "I need to borrow Max for a few minutes." She steered Max away from Allie and Grady. Max tried to unhook his arm from Luna's grasp, but for such a slender girl, she was *very* forceful. "Now, Max," she said, "I want you to tell me *all* about this time-thingy of yours. I think time travel is *totally* fascinating!"

Grady turned to Allie and said, "Come on, let's find Toby."

Allie stood still, watching Max and Luna. "'I think time travel is *totally* fascinating!'" she mimicked, an angry flush in her freckled cheeks. "That Luna Skyes is so *pushy!*"

In the middle of the lawn, under the mirror ball, sat Max's old Volkswagen Beetle. It was ugly, orange, and dented all over, but Max and Allie had decorated it with colored streamers and silver helium balloons. Sparkling lights danced upon its bent chrome and buckled roof.

Max had turned the old VW Beetle into a time machine that he called "Timebender." Max, Grady, Allie, and Toby Brubaker had gone back in time in that old car. On that trip, they were almost eaten by a dinosaur and enslaved by a dragon—but they also met a wonderful golden being named Gavriyel.

"So this is Time Blender!" Luna said, clutching Max's arm. "I think that's the *cutest* name for a time machine!"

"It's Time*bender*," Max said.

"Whatever," she said. "I think time travel is just too cool for words."

"Yeah, right," Max said. "You don't believe it really works. Everyone thinks it's just a gag."

"Oh, no, Max!" Luna said. "I really believe in it! I think your story about dinosaurs and traveling through space is just the most wonderful adventure I've ever heard! Can we sit in it?"

"Well," Max said, hesitating. "Okay." He opened the passenger door and let her in, then he got in behind the steering wheel.

Luna looked around at the broken windows, the ratty upholstery, the cracked dashboard—and she wrinkled her nose. "It doesn't smell very good," she said.

"I know," Max said. "It's had that smell ever since it got sunk in the mud in the Cretaceous Period."

"Oh," Luna said. "I thought there would be, like, lights and dials and stuff."

"Nope," Max said. "It's really pretty simple. The whole thing is powered by flashlight batteries. See those calculators on the dashboard? They're held on with plain old duct tape—nothing fancy. I rewired those calculators to show the time coordinates—and I came up with some improve-ments. See there? Those new displays let me set the geo-graphic coordinates as well as the time coordinates."

Luna yawned.

"Sorry," he said, reaching for the door handle. "This is boring you. I'd better go—"

Luna grabbed his arm. "Don't go!" she said suddenly. "Max, don't you wonder why I'm suddenly so interested in you, and in Time Blender?"

"Well—"

"You see, Max," Luna said, "I used to think you were, well, kind of geeky. You know, all brainy and shy and—" She paused, groping for words.

"Uncool," Max said.

"Yeah," Luna said. "But now I see you are *way* cool."

"I am?"

"Totally," she said. "I mean, even your name is cool—Max McCrane. It sounds so strong and courageous. It's the perfect name for a time traveler!" Luna paused, as if she expected Max to say something nice about her name.

Max shifted uncomfortably. "Well, uh," he said, fumbling for words, "you have a really interesting name, too—Luna."

She smiled. "You like it? I made it up myself. I wanted a name that sounds mysterious and fascinating. You know what my parents named me? *Laura.*" She wrinkled her nose. "Can you believe that? Laura! It's so—"

"I think Laura's a pretty name," said Max.

"Oh?" Luna seemed pleased. "Well, you can call me Laura. It'll be your secret name for me."

Max coughed. Her perfume irritated his asthma. "Luna—Laura," he said, "I've really got to go." He opened the door and made his escape—just barely. He felt her fingernails rake his arm as he slipped out of the car.

"Max!" she called after him.

Max looked through the broken window. "Yeah?"

"What's your sign?"

"My what?"

"Your sign! I'm a Gemini, with a Virgo moon and Libra rising."

"Oh," Max said. "Well, I think astrology is kind of stupid." He reached beneath the collar of his shirt and pulled out something he wore on a gold neck chain. "That's my sign," he said. It was a simple gold cross.

Luna looked disappointed. "Oh," she said. "You're one of *those*."

"Yeah," Max said. "Well, I've got to go!" And he took off.

Still gripping his bag of tricks, Toby kept to the shadows by the walnut grove and made his way toward the huge old McCrane House. He had spotted Grady looking for him over by the picnic tables, then had almost bumped into Allie coming from the opposite direction. Only a quick detour through the darkened walnut grove let him slip past without being seen.

The old Victorian house loomed up out of the darkness. Toby had heard weird tales about the old house. Rumors said it was haunted. There were stories of people who had entered the house—and were never heard from again. There was even a tale of *treasure* hidden inside the house—and *that* was the story that had captured Toby's imagination. After all, everyone knew that Max's dad, Dr. Oswald McCrane, was worth millions. That screw-loose inventor spent money by the truckload on his crazy contraptions. What if the rumors were true? What if Dr. McCrane's millions really were stuffed away in those walls in the form of gold, jewels, and old coins?

Maybe those rumors were just a lot of talk—but then again, maybe not. If there really was treasure stashed in the walls, now was Toby's chance to find out for himself.

He paused behind a gnarled tree, making sure no one was watching. Then he crossed into the shadows of the house, heading for the back porch—

Ooof!

He tripped over something in the dark and landed flat on his face. Swearing under his breath, Toby scrambled to his feet. Looking down, he saw what had tripped him: a black electrical cord. The cord snaked up the steps to the back porch. There, next to the back door, was an electrical outlet. A hand-lettered sign over the outlet read:

Power for Party Lights!!
DO NOT TOUCH!!

Perfect! With one yank on that cord, Toby could stop the music and plunge the party into darkness!

He dashed up the steps and onto the porch, setting the bag by his feet. Then, with a wicked grin on his pasty face, Toby reached for the cord.

Max, Grady, and Allie all came together by the picnic tables. "Did you see him?" Max asked.

"No," Allie said.

"Me neither," Grady said. "Did you?"

"Nope," Max answered glumly.

And *that's* when it happened.

3

THE THRESHOLD OF TIME

Toby gripped the cord with both hands and pulled.

Boom! The explosive sound made Toby jump.

But he was even more surprised moments later when he realized that the party was still going on. The lights and lasers still electrified the night. The music still blasted. People still talked and laughed. And now, something new—

A multicolored snowstorm of confetti and streamers fluttered down out of the sky. The *Boom!* that had startled Toby was the firing of a confetti cannon. He looked at the disconnected cord in his hand. Pulling that plug should have shut down the party—but it didn't.

Toby didn't have time to stop and figure it out. Snatching up the bag, he flung open the back door of the McCrane House and disappeared inside.

It was still snowing confetti when Max, Allie, and Grady reached the back porch. They found Dr. McCrane already standing there, holding the end of an electrical cord. When he saw Max, Allie, and Grady approaching, Max's dad said, "You were right, Max. It must have been the Brubaker boy."

"What happened?" Grady said. "What's with all the confetti?"

"Something Dad and I invented," Max explained. "We call it a Toby Detector."

"It was Max's idea," Dr. McCrane said. "If the cord is pulled out of the socket, the current is interrupted, triggering a relay that fires a confetti cannon on the third-floor balcony."

"Toby found it," Max said, "and he did just what Dad and I thought he might do."

Allie pointed to the cord. "Well, if that's not the power cord for the party," she said, "where does the power come from?"

"Batteries," Max said. "All the lights, the fog machines, the stereo—everything is powered by batteries."

"What about Toby?" Grady said. "Where did he go?"

"I don't know," Dr. McCrane said. "He was gone when I got here."

"He must have gone into the house," Allie said. "If he'd headed toward the lawn, one of us would have seen him."

"Dad," Max said, "you'd better stay with the laptop. The three of us will go inside and find Toby."

"Okay," Dr. McCrane said. "But be careful. Looks like this Brubaker boy is nothing but trouble."

Toby found himself in a hallway with many doors. The old house seemed to go on forever. *This place really creeps me out!* Toby thought. *Dude, a guy could get totally lost in here!*

Finally, he reached the entryway at the front of the house. There was a staircase to his right, the front door straight ahead, doorways leading to other rooms—

And one locked room with the key in the door.

Toby unlocked the door, walked in, flipped on the lights, and closed the door softly behind him. The room looked like a library. The walls were lined with books, and there was antique furniture all around.

Then Toby saw the Doorway.

It was built into the wall on the far side of the room—a door of inlaid oak, a doorframe richly carved and accented with gold, a series of clear quartz crystals set into the frame. To Toby's mind, the crystals looked like huge diamonds. *The hidden treasure!* he thought.

He rushed toward the Doorway, but in his haste, he tripped over the edge of the Persian rug and went sprawling.

The bag flew out of his hands. Something popped out of the bag and rolled away.

Toby swore. His knee throbbed. It was the second time in less than five minutes that he had fallen on his face. He clambered to his feet, picked up the bag, and limped to the Doorway.

Then he saw the eyeball.

It was a glow-in-the-dark eyeball like the ones he had put on the pizza. It had popped out of his bag when he tripped. It sat on the floor in front of the Doorway, staring at him.

Toby picked it up, but in the next instant, the eyeball was forgotten. All Toby could think about was the Doorway. He stared greedily at its huge, diamondlike crystals of transparent quartz. He set the bag down and grabbed the door handle with one hand and tugged. The door wouldn't budge. He needed both hands.

He looked for a place to set the eyeball—then he noticed a cup-shaped receptacle of blackened metal that jutted from the doorpost. He set the eyeball in the receptacle—

And something strange happened: The crystals in the Doorway lit up with a cool, liquid radiance.

Toby backed away from the Doorway. Had he set off an alarm that guarded the hidden treasure?

Well, what if he had? That only proved there was something worth stealing on the other side of the door! If the Doorway had huge, sparkling diamonds on it (at least

Toby *thought* the quartz crystals were diamonds), then the treasure it guarded must be more valuable than he could imagine!

He grasped the handle with both hands. Still it refused to budge. In his frustration, he kicked the door. Then he kicked it again. And again.

◎ ◎ ◎

A thousand years earlier . . .

In an alchemist's laboratory, high in a castle tower, two men stood before the golden Doorway to the future. One man was the alchemist himself, dressed in dark robes. The other was a king.

"Your Majesty," the old alchemist said, bowing deeply and making a sweeping flourish of his robes. "Here is the device I told you about. I call it the Doorway of the Ages."

The king was a hard-muscled man of about fifty, with shoulder-length black hair that grayed at the temples, eyes of steel-blue, and a strong, smooth chin that seemed chiseled in marble. His crown was ornate and bedecked with jewels—a glittering symbol of the king's huge ego. He wore a blood-red tunic and black breeches. At his side was a sword of fine Damascus steel.

The Doorway shone in the morning sunlight that streamed through the windows. The king eyed the Doorway with a skeptical frown, then walked all the way around it. "Seems an odd place for a door," he said at last. "It doesn't lead anyplace."

"True," the old alchemist said, "this Doorway does not lead to another *place*. It leads to another *time*. I've walked through it."

"Oh?" the king said with a raised eyebrow. "When?"

"Yesterday," the alchemist said. "The Doorway transported me to a room of the future, a kind of library filled with books, the knowledge of ages yet to come—see?" The old man handed a book to the king.

The king flipped through the book and was astonished. This was no hand-lettered manuscript. He had never seen a machine-printed book before. He had never seen a photograph before. Yet here, in this strange book, were color photographs of astonishing detail—images of rockets launching skyward on plumes of fire, buildings exploding, cities in ruins. The king hardly knew what to make of all those strange and baffling images. He closed the book and read the title:

Rockets and Modern Warfare
by
Thaxter O. Butterworth

"I have spent the past day and night studying that book," the old alchemist said. "It is a book of weapons, my king— weapons of the future."

The king thought for a moment. "This library you visited," he said, handing the book to the alchemist, "must have contained hundreds of books—yet you brought back only one?"

"I was interrupted by a boy," the alchemist said. "He was a strange-looking lad, with a pair of round glass windows perched on his nose that he looked through. He saw me, then he locked the door and called for help. I had to flee quickly—"

A loud *thump!* startled both men.

The noise came from the Doorway. It sounded as if someone was kicking the door from the other side.

There was a second kick, then a third.

The king put his hand on his sword, ready to draw steel.

The door shuddered and shook. Someone was trying to open the door from the other side—but both men knew there was no one there!

The third kick hurt Toby's foot. *Dude,* he thought, *that door is solid! I won't get anywhere by kicking it.*

In his frustration, Toby grabbed the door handle with both hands. He pulled, yanked, and tugged at the door. It refused to open.

Max, Allie, and Grady heard *Whump! . . . Whump! . . . Whump!* as they rushed down the hallway.

"What was that?" Allie asked.

"Sounded like someone knocking on a door," Grady said.

"Sounded more like someone *kicking* a door," Max said. "Come on! This way!"

The king took a step closer to the Doorway. Someone was definitely pulling on the door from the other side.

He walked around to the side of the doorframe and looked at the backside of the door. There was no one there. Still, the door continued to shudder and shake.

He went to the front of the door, placed his hand against it—and pushed.

Toby pulled—and the door came unstuck! It was as if someone had pushed from the other side. He staggered back in amazement.

The Doorway stood open, but Toby saw nothing but blackness beyond. It was as if a dense black veil hung over the opening.

He took a fearful step closer. *The treasure has to be in*

there, he thought. *Maybe there's a light switch beyond the door.*

Toby paused at the threshold of the Doorway, his heart hammering in his throat. Cautiously, he reached out into the darkness, groping for a light switch—

Something grabbed his hand and *pulled,* yanking him off his feet, dragging him through the Doorway, into the darkness.

Max, Allie, and Grady arrived at the entryway.

"Where could Toby be?" Allie said. "There are a zillion rooms in this house."

The doorbell chimed. Max, Allie, and Grady jumped halfway out of their skins. They turned and looked at the front door. Through the stained-glass panel of the door, they saw people.

Max opened the door and peered out. A crowd jammed the porch. Most were delivery guys carrying stacks of cardboard pizza boxes. The one closest to the door said, "Is this the McCrane House?"

"Yeah," Max said.

"Got an order here for ten pizzas."

"Me, too," said another delivery guy.

Max blinked in astonishment. There were pizza guys swarming up the walk. In the street in front of the house were taxicabs, a few plumbers' vans, and an exterminator's truck with a big plastic cockroach on top.

"What should I do with these pizzas?" asked the first delivery guy.

"Go around to the backyard," Max said. "Ask for Dr. McCrane." Max closed the door.

Allie was fuming. "Oh! That Toby!"

Grady shook his head. "It's Jodi's party all over again."

"Come on," Max said.

They checked the music room, the billiard room, the dining room, the parlor—

But when Max checked the door to the study, he knew something wasn't right. The door was closed, but unlocked— and Max *knew* his dad had locked it the night before. Max flung the door open and jumped back—but the book-lined room was empty.

Across the room, the Doorway stood open.

A strange man had Toby in a viselike grip—*a man,* Toby thought, *who was costumed as a king.*

"It's the boy!" said another man, a much older man dressed in a wizard's costume. The old man peered into Toby's face. "Wait—it's not the same boy! The other boy was lean and had thick brown hair and wore round glass eye-windows on his face. This boy's hair is cropped almost to the skin—perhaps as a punishment for some misdeed, eh? Tell me, boy—where did you come from, and how did you get through the Doorway?"

"Dude, let go of me!" Toby yelled—and he delivered a vicious kick to the shin of the king.

With a howl of pain, the king released Toby and grabbed his throbbing leg. Toby dashed away from the king, past the old alchemist, and around to the far side of the laboratory table.

The king glared at Toby. "Lad," he growled, "I'll flay your hide for that!" He hobbled toward the left side of the table. The alchemist moved around the right side.

"Don't let him get to the Doorway!" the alchemist shouted.

Then Toby saw the open window. It looked like his only chance for escape. He dashed around the end of the lab table, launching himself at the window. As he reached it, he batted something out of his way that was perched upon the window sill—a glass beaker containing a greenish stone.

"No!" the alchemist shouted.

But it was too late. The glass beaker and the moonstone were already tumbling out the window.

Toby was halfway through the window when he looked down and saw a long drop to the ground below. He had assumed the window was at ground level—but now he was looking down from the height of a ten-story building.

He saw the glass beaker and the moonstone fall—*splish! splash!*—into a water-filled moat outside a castle wall.

Toby let out a scream!

Then he felt a powerful hand grip him by the leg and pull him back inside. Toby looked up into the fierce scowl of the king.

"I just saved your wretched hide, lad," the king said. "But when I'm done with you, you'll be begging for death!"

Max hurried to the Doorway, followed closely by Grady and Allie. "Guys, look!" Max said, pointing. Light shone from the quartz crystals in the doorframe. Beyond the open Doorway was a strange inky blackness that swallowed all light.

All three felt it: a thrill of fear, a tingle of dread. Something horrible lay across that threshold.

"Hey, what's that?" Grady said. He reached out and snatched something from the metal receptacle in the doorpost. The thing in his hand was soft and squishy. The moment he removed it, the crystals went dark.

"Look!" He held it up for Max and Allie to see.

"A glow-in-the-dark eyeball!" Allie said. "Like the ones Toby put on the pizzas!"

"He was here," Max said.

Allie pointed to the brass receptacle. "Did you see what happened when Grady took it out of that thing?"

"Yeah, the crystals went dark," Grady said.

"And look," Max said, pointing through the open doorway. The inky blackness was gone. In its place was an ordinary closet with stacks of cardboard boxes sitting on the floor.

"Guys," Allie said, "this is really creepy."

"Yeah," Max said. "But we have to find out what happened to Toby."

"Then let's do this," Grady said. He put the eyeball back in the metal receptacle. Instantly, the quartz crystals lit up again. Beyond the open Doorway, the boxes and the closet disappeared. In their place was a black hole of darkness.

Max looked grim. "Toby went through there," he said. "He's in there now. This Doorway is a device of some kind. It's a Doorway to some other place, maybe some other dimension. It looks like it draws power from phosphorescent light—the light given off by glow-in-the-dark eyeballs."

Then Max remembered the previous night's mystery. Had the menacing stranger left the room through this Doorway? Max hadn't mentioned the intruder to Grady and Allie, and there was no time to explain it now. But Max *had* to know—not just what happened to Toby, but what happened to the stranger.

"Let's check it out," Max said.

"No way," Allie said. "This is too scary. Can't we, like, get your dad to help us?"

"There's no time for that," said Max. "Toby has a big head start on us. If we're going to find him, we can't just stand around. We've got to *do* something!"

Allie glanced nervously at the darkness in the Doorway. "Maybe he didn't go in there after all," she said.

"He's in there," Max said firmly. "I have an idea. I'll poke my head through to see what's beyond that darkness. You guys hold on to me. If anything goes wrong, just pull me back."

Allie rolled her eyes and took hold of Max's arm. "This is *such* a bad idea."

Grady bent down and wrapped his arms around Max's legs. Max prayed silently—then he leaned into the darkness of the Doorway.

The king gripped Toby by his collar and lifted him off the floor with one hand. "This lad," he said, "must be taught to respect the shinbones of a king! Perhaps a flogging in the courtyard will do him some good."

Toby's eyes widened as he looked toward the Doorway. "McCrane!" he hollered. "Dude! Get me out of here!"

The king turned and looked toward the Doorway. Out of the darkness of the open Doorway, a boy's head floated— a boy with brown hair and round-lensed eyeglasses. The king, of course, had never seen eyeglasses before—but he remembered how Doctor Delyrius had described the boy who surprised him in the library: "a strange-looking lad, with a pair of round glass windows perched on his nose." The floating head in the Doorway certainly matched the Doctor's description.

The alchemist took a step toward Max's hovering head. "You!" he shouted.

Max's eyes widened. "You!" he said.

The king flung Toby aside. In three strides, he reached the Doorway and grabbed Max by the shoulders.

Max shouted to his friends, "Pull me back! Pull me back!"

But the sound of Max's voice didn't carry across the time barrier.

Then Grady and Allie felt something yank at Max, nearly pulling him out of their grasp. Allie screamed and clung harder to Max's arm. Grady tightened his grip on Max's legs. Allie and Grady refused to let go, but they couldn't pull him back. First, Allie lost her footing, then Grady—

And all three tumbled into the darkness between the centuries.

4

THE HALL OF THE DRAGON KING

The king thought he had ahold of *one* boy.

Suddenly, out of the Doorway tumbled the brown-haired boy, a black-skinned boy, and a red-haired girl. The impact knocked the king over backward. He landed on his back with all three kids on top of him.

Allie was the first on her feet. "Toby!" she called, rushing to Toby's side. She tugged at him, and Toby got up, looking around uncertainly.

Max and Grady clambered off the king—but Max instantly found himself in the grip of bony fingers. He looked up and saw the bearded face of the old alchemist. Despite his age, the old man was strong. "Let go of me!" Max yelled, struggling.

"Come on, guys!" Grady shouted. "Back through the Doorway!" But the king snatched Grady's foot, pulling him off his feet.

Then the king leaped up and drew his sword, blocking Allie and Toby from the Doorway. Allie screamed and jumped back, pulling Toby's arm.

"Nobody move!" the king ordered through clenched teeth. "All of you—up against that wall." With his sword point, he indicated the wall farthest from the Doorway.

Max glanced desperately toward the Doorway, their only hope for escape. Then he looked at the king's sword—and his eyes widened at the sight of that shining steel blade with its razor-keen edge. There was no way he or his friends could get to the Doorway.

Still gripped by the old alchemist, Max looked at Grady, who was climbing to his feet. Max knew what his friend was thinking. He saw it in Grady's eyes and the way the boy's athletic body was tensed: Grady was thinking of rushing the king, sword and all! "Grady, don't," Max said nervously.

Grady glanced at Max, his face hard, his body coiled.

"We've got to do what he says," Max said, "or somebody will get hurt."

Grady hesitated.

"Listen to your friend, lad," the king said in a threatening tone, swinging the sword in Grady's direction.

The fight went out of Grady. "Okay, Max," he said.

The alchemist released Max from his grip. Max and Grady reluctantly trudged over to where Allie and Toby waited against the wall.

"I," the king said, his face twitching with rage, "am

King Wyvern of Gyle—Sovereign of the Realm, Defender of the Serpenfane, and Seigneur of the Order of the Knights of Draconis Argentus! Now, I don't know what uncivilized country you urchins come from, but in the Kingdom of Gyle, no one is permitted to kick, trip, pummel, or assault the royal person of the king! If one of you guttersnipes so much as touches the hem of my royal cloak, *it will cost you your head!*"

The four time travelers nodded, wide-eyed.

"And I," the old alchemist said, "am Doctor Herendus Delyrius—Artium Baccalaureus, Praefectus Magnus, and Magister of the Hidden Arts and Alchemic Sciences."

"I'm pleased to meet you, sirs," Max said, remembering his manners. "We're—"

"Who you and your friends are," Doctor Delyrius said, "is of no importance. The question is: What shall we do with you?"

"Let us go back through the Doorway, please," Max said. "We want to go home."

"No!" the king snapped. "That Doorway is a menace. I'll shut it before anything else tumbles out!" He reached into the darkness of the Doorway, found the door handle, and pulled.

"No!" Doctor Delyrius said. He lunged for the door— but he was too late. The door clicked shut and the crystals went dark. "Look what you've done!" the Doctor groaned.

"What are you babbling about?" King Wyvern asked.

"When you closed that door," the alchemist said, "you broke the connection to the future."

"Just make the Doorway work again!" the king said.

"I can't!" the alchemist said. "Not without the moonstone." The alchemist pointed at Toby. "And *he* knocked the moonstone into the moat! Without that stone, the Doorway is useless!"

"Max!" Allie whispered. "What are they talking about?"

"I'm not sure," Max whispered back. "But it looks like we're stuck in the past—and there's no way to get back."

King Wyvern and Doctor Delyrius marched the four time travelers down the stairs and handed them over to the tower guards. "Take charge of these ruffians," the king commanded. "Take them to the great hall in the palace." Then the king and Doctor Delyrius left them.

The guards marched Max, Allie, Grady, and Toby across the grassy courtyard to the palace. As the four were led into the king's palace, they were amazed at what they saw: On the walls hung colorful tapestries and paintings, depicting scenes of epic battles. A magnificent chandelier with a hundred burning candles was suspended over the center of the hall. The candles' glow shone on eye-dazzling treasures of gold, silver, and precious gems, stacked wherever space could be found. There were statues and figurines, plates and goblets, vases and decanters, and open chests overflowing with jewelry and coins.

The four time travelers were led to one end of the hall

and held at spearpoint by several guards. Despite the danger they were in, Toby's green eyes glittered greedily at the sight of all that treasure.

In the center of the great hall of King Wyvern was a long table of honey-colored oak. At the center of the table was a silver statue.

Allie gasped. "Max," she said with a nudge. "Look!" Max looked where Allie pointed and saw a statue of a winged, four-legged serpentlike creature.

The Silver Dragon.

The creature's snakelike body and batlike wings were fashioned of mirror-polished silver, and its eyes were blood-red rubies. It looked exactly like the *real* fire-breathing dragon that Max, Allie, and Grady had battled on their previous journey back in time. The sight of that statue filled them with horror.

In another part of the palace, King Wyvern knelt on the floor in his contemplation room. Whenever King Wyvern had an important decision to make, he would go to the contemplation room and get on his knees before a statue of the Silver Dragon.

As he knelt, there came a knock on the door. "Enter," King Wyvern said.

The door opened and Doctor Delyrius came in. "Your

knights have been summoned to the great hall," Doctor Delyrius said, "along with Lady Galatea." He turned to leave.

The king said, "Don't go, Doctor."

"Yes, my king?"

"I have been thinking about those four bratlings. Their arrival is a most remarkable occurrence. I believe the Dragon has a reason for bringing them here from the distant future. Perhaps they possess useful knowledge, hmm?"

"Perhaps," the Doctor said.

King Wyvern stood and turned to face the Doctor—and he suddenly drew his sword. The Doctor backed away. The king held the blade in the air before him.

"My sword grows restless," he said, admiring its bright blue steel. "It has been weeks since we defeated King Aticus of the West Umbrians. I am weary of peace. We have conquered our enemies to the south, east, and west. It is time to march against our enemies to the north."

"But, sire," the Doctor said, "we have no enemies to the north."

A cruel smile twisted the king's lips. "We will."

"Then you will attack the Kingdom of Elysia? You would break the peace treaty with Queen Marielle?"

"A treaty," the king said, "is just a piece of parchment. I am the Dragon King, Doctor, and I serve the Silver Dragon. My empire was not built with ink stains on parchment, but with bloodstains on cold steel."

"Yes, Your Majesty," the Doctor said.

"Come, Doctor," King Wyvern said. "Let us go to the great hall."

"They have images and statues of the Silver Dragon," Allie said. "It's almost as if they *worship* that evil creature! What do you think it means?"

"It means," Grady said, "that our coming here was no accident. There are too many coincidences. It's got to be part of a plan—the Eternal Plan. I think the Creator must have a reason for bringing us here."

"Grady's right," Max said. "The same evil we fought before is here—and we have to fight it again."

"You mean the Silver Dragon is *here?*" Allie asked.

"The Dragon!" Toby exclaimed, his eyes alight. While the mere mention of the Silver Dragon filled the others with dread, it filled Toby with a feeling of expectation and wicked delight.

"If the Dragon is here," Allie continued, "doesn't that mean we'll have to go through that same battle all over again?"

"Same enemy," Grady said, "but a different battle. I don't think we'll face an actual dragon this time. Instead, the dragon is working through people like King Wyvern and that weird old Doctor Delyrius."

"Dude!" Toby shouted. "Get your hands off me!"

Max, Allie, and Grady turned and saw one of the spear-wielding guards running his hand over the logo on the back of Toby's blue long-sleeve tee shirt.

"Easy, Toby," said Allie. "The guy's just curious."

"Yeah," said Max. "Remember, these people have never seen designer tee shirts or overalls or tennis shoes or eye-glasses or any of that stuff. We must look pretty strange to them."

The double doors at the east end of the hall swung open, and King Wyvern and Doctor Delyrius entered the hall. Then the doors at the west end swung open, and a woman entered, followed by twenty knights in chain mail, with swords at their sides. The king went to the head of the table. Doctor Delyrius took his place on the king's right hand, and the woman on the king's left. The knights found their places all along the table.

"Stand there," a guard told the four captives. Max, Allie, Grady, and Toby trudged to the foot of the table and faced the king at the far end.

"I have convened this council," King Wyvern said, "to decide the fate of these four prisoners. They have come to us from a thousand years in the future."

An astonished murmur arose among the knights.

"These ruffians," King Wyvern continued, "have physically assaulted your king."

An even more astonished murmur arose.

"That's not true!" Max protested. "It was an accident! We didn't even know he was a king!"

"Silence, scoundrel!" the king said. "Do not speak unless you are spoken to!" He turned to his knights. "Now, under the laws of the Kingdom of Gyle, the crime of assaulting the royal personage is punishable by death—"

All four youths felt a chill of fear.

"But," the king continued, "I have chosen to be merciful. I will give these four guttersnipes a chance to prove themselves useful. Doctor Delyrius, milady, noble knights—who among you is willing to take one of these whelps as your squire or apprentice?"

Doctor Delyrius rose to his feet. "You, the one with the round windows on your face," he said, pointing to Max. "What is your name?"

"Max McCrane, sir," he said.

"Well, Max McCrane," the Doctor said, "we first met in a room filled with books. I only got a chance to look at a few of those books, but from what I could see, they were filled with scientific knowledge. May I assume that you have some knowledge of the science of the future?"

"The future? You mean your future and my present?" Max wasn't sure where this was leading. "Well—"

"Max is the smartest kid at Victor Appleton Middle School," Allie said. "When it comes to science, he's—"

"Allie!" Max hissed. "Don't help me!"

Allie put her hand to her mouth. "Oops! Sorry, Max!"

Doctor Delyrius turned to King Wyvern. "I find the lad acceptable," he said. "If he is as clever as the girl claims, he may prove useful." The Doctor sat down.

The king nodded. "Are any of my knights in need of a squire?"

One of the knights stood up—a young man with shoulder-length black hair, steely blue eyes, and a cruel smirk. "With training, the ebony-skinned fellow might make a fine swordsman." He nodded to Grady. "Your name, lad?"

"Grady Stubblefield," Grady said.

"Very well," King Wyvern said. "Grady of the Stubble Field, you shall become the squire of Sir Guy of Scymbria."

The king nodded to Allie. "And your name, lass?"

"My name is Allie O'Dell, Your Majesty," she answered, trembling.

"Allie o' the Dell," the king said. "I place you in the keeping of the noblest lady of my court—Lady Galatea. Milady?"

Lady Galatea stood. She was dressed in a black gown, tied at the waist with a cord of red silk, with a black cloak over her shoulders. A wimple of black cloth framed her face and was drawn into folds beneath her chin. Her lips were a thin slash of crimson. Her eyes were dark, almost black. She was beautiful, but it was a severe and unhappy beauty, and Allie sensed that this woman must have suffered a deep sorrow in her life.

"Well, that leaves only one of these young wretches unclaimed," said King Wyvern. "Surely one of my knights will take the lumpish, beady-eyed lad as his squire."

No knight spoke. An awkward silence passed. A look of impatience grew on the king's face. "Sir Osbert," the king said impatiently, "I believe you would like to volunteer, would you not?"

The old knight rose reluctantly to his feet. He was a tall, barrel-chested man with a prominent nose, a gray handle-bar moustache, and a long battle scar that started at his right ear and sliced down his cheek to the point of his chin. "Your Majesty," the old knight said in a deep, resentful growl, "I would like to volunteer to take the swine-faced boy as my squire."

"Hey!" Toby said, frowning. "Who's he calling 'swine-faced'?"

"State your name, swine-faced boy!" the king roared.

Toby's knees shook. "My name is Toby Brubaker, Your Royaltyness, sir."

The king frowned. "That's a strange name. Toby . . . Brew-Baker? Just what is your family trade? Is your father a brewer or a baker?"

"My old man?" said Toby, a look of bafflement on his face. "He's a trucker."

Now it was the king's turn to look baffled. "Very well, Toby, son of Brew-Baker the Trucker, you shall become the squire of brave Sir Osbert."

"Doctor Delyrius, noble knights, gentle lady," King Wyvern said, "these grubby young gamins are yours to instruct as you see fit. Teach them and prepare them for the dark days ahead."

The Doctor, the two knights, and Lady Galatea left the

long table and came to the side of the room where the four young time travelers stood.

"Wait!" Allie said. "Stop! You can't separate us!"

"Allie's right," Max said. "We're staying together!"

Doctor Delyrius snatched Max's wrist. "Come with me, boy—and no argument!"

Allie reached for Max, but Sir Osbert stepped between them. "Max," Allie called, trying not to cry.

"It'll be okay, Allie," Max called as the Doctor pulled him through a doorway and out of the hall. "Don't lose faith!"

"Max is right," Grady said. "We have to go with these people and do what they say. But it'll work out."

"A wise attitude, lad," Sir Guy of Scymbria said. "Come along."

"And you," Sir Osbert said, shoving Toby in the back. "Come with me."

Lady Galatea placed her hand on Allie's arm. "Come, Allie O'Dell," she said primly. "I have many questions to ask you. . . ."

5

THE RAGE OF DOCTOR DELYRIUS

Max sat on a three-legged stool in the Doctor's laboratory. Behind him was the golden Doorway, gleaming in the afternoon sunlight from the open window. Doctor Delyrius took a book from the laboratory table and showed it to Max: *Rockets and Modern Warfare*.

Max glared at the old man. "That book belongs to my dad," Max said. "You *stole* it."

"I take what I want," Doctor Delyrius said, "and I let nothing get in my way. Do you understand?" There was a note of threat in the Doctor's voice.

"Yes, sir," Max replied.

"Good," the Doctor said. "This book contains words I'm not familiar with—words like *oxidant*, *nitric acid*, and *hypersonic*. Do you know what those words mean?"

Max said nothing.

"You *do* know," Doctor Delyrius said. "I can see it in your eyes." He chuckled. "You cannot hide the truth from Doctor Delyrius."

"What do you want?" Max asked.

"I want you to interpret this book for me," the Doctor said. "Explain its secrets to me."

"So you can build rockets like the ones in the book?"

"Exactly," the Doctor said.

"What are you going to do with rockets?" Max asked. "Blow up castles? Kill people?"

"You *are* a clever lad," the Doctor said.

Max thought quickly. He had built model rockets with his dad as a hobby. He knew a lot about rockets—but he refused to let his knowledge be used to help Doctor Delyrius, King Wyvern, or the Silver Dragon.

"I won't help you," Max said.

Doctor Delyrius smiled wickedly. "Oh, I think you will. You care about your friends—and you wouldn't want something *terrible* to happen to them, would you?"

Max knew he faced an impossible choice. People would be hurt no matter which way he decided. *What should I do, God?* he prayed. *What should I do?*

@ @ @

Lady Galatea led Allie out of the palace and across the central courtyard of the castle. When Allie had first seen her from across the palace hall, the lady had seemed cold and forbidding. But now, as they walked side by side, Allie sensed that the lady was not really as stern and forbidding as she had seemed at first—just very, very sad. Allie even thought she detected a glint of kindness in the lady's eyes.

As they walked across the courtyard, Allie looked around. She had been fascinated by castles ever since reading *The Crimson Dragon of Castle Morbidus* by J. Farthington Frimby—one of her favorite books. "Milady," she said, "what is this castle called?"

"This," the lady replied, "is Castle Serpenfane."

Allie could see that Castle Serpenfane was laid out in a square, with high, cylinder-shaped towers at each corner. The palace of King Wyvern was behind her, and the front gate of the castle lay ahead of her, dominated by a massive gatehouse. Watchmen lined the turrets atop the gatehouse. Banners were hung around the castle walls—red and black banners emblazoned with the image of the Silver Dragon.

"I have a room in the top of that tower," the lady said, pointing to the tower left of the gatehouse. "You'll be staying with me." She gave Allie a curious look. "Is it true, as the king said, that you and your friends have come from a thousand years in the future?"

"It's true," Allie said. "Pretty weird, huh? Doctor Delyrius built this Doorway—some kind of time-travel thingy. Now it doesn't work, so we're stuck here." She looked around—then pointed to the castle tower to the right of the gatehouse. "Isn't that the Doctor's tower?"

"Yes," the lady said. "His laboratory is at the top."

"Poor Max," Allie said. "I guess he's up there with the Doctor right now."

"I suppose he is," the lady said.

Allie pointed to their left at a beautiful building of ornately carved stone. "What is that building?"

"The chapel," the lady answered. "It is boarded up and no longer used."

"No longer used?" Allie said, surprised.

Lady Galatea stopped. "See that broken capstone on the roof? That is where the stone cross was torn down. The chapel was closed by order of King Wyvern, and no one has gone inside for ten years."

"But why?"

Lady Galatea did not answer. Instead, she gazed across the courtyard. "Look," she said, pointing.

Allie saw various people—young squires running errands, guards at doorways, two tradesmen lugging a wooden barrel between them, and some girls filling pitchers at a well—then she saw the scene the lady was pointing out to her: Grady and Sir Guy of Scymbria were marching across the court-yard, followed closely by Toby and Sir Osbert.

It broke Allie's heart to see them. Grady walked straight and tall, but Toby stumbled as he walked, and looked pale and scared.

"Where are they going?" Allie asked.

The lady pointed to a row of two-story buildings along the far wall. "On the bottom floor are the blacksmith's shop and the stables. The upper story is the barracks, where the knights and squires live. Your friends will live in those barracks and train as squires."

"What's a squire?" Allie asked.

"A servant of a knight," Lady Galatea said. "The squires train with the knights."

"You mean Grady and Toby will be learning about swordfighting and chivalry and all of that?"

"Of course," the lady said, "and so will you."

Allie looked startled. "Me!"

"I am a warrioress," Lady Galatea explained. "After the death of my husband, I learned swordcraft—and I have offered my blade in service to King Wyvern. Now you shall be my squiress, and I shall teach you everything I know about the craft of war."

"But I've read books about the Middle Ages!" Allie said. "Women don't carry swords. What about the Code of Knighthood? Knights take a vow to protect women—not ride with them into war!"

"Ah," the lady said, "the Code of Knighthood. That quaint custom is observed by *Christian* knights. The Kingdom of Gyle is not a Christian kingdom, and King Wyvern is not a Christian king. Come along."

Lady Galatea continued walking toward the tower. As

Allie hurried to keep up, her mind worked quickly. Here, a woman could be a warrior, in violation of the Code of Knighthood. Here, the king worshiped a dragon. And here, the chapel was shuttered and deserted, its cross torn down.

Something was very wrong at Castle Serpenfane.

Toby and Grady looked around the stable. The horses had been removed from the stalls. Each stall had a layer of straw on the floor, and the straw was matted with muck.

"Here's where your training begins," Sir Osbert said in a deep growl.

"Take these," Sir Guy said. He gave each boy a rough wooden pole with sticks bound to one end in a fan shape.

"What's this?" Toby asked, examining the tool.

"A muck rake," Sir Guy said. He pointed to the stable floor. "Now, muck out these stalls."

"Start in the far corner," Sir Osbert said. "See that nothing gets missed."

So, Toby and Grady began mucking out the stalls. It was disgusting work. The muck stank and smeared the boys' shoes. Dust and straw particles swirled in the air and went up their noses. After a few minutes, Toby threw down his muck rake. "Dude, this is whack!" he said. "I'm not doing this anymore."

Sir Osbert cuffed Toby with the back of his hand.

"Ow!" Toby whimpered, rubbing his stinging cheek.

"Lesson one," growled Sir Osbert, his gray walrus moustache twitching. "Do what you're told, no complaining."

Toby went back to work.

◎ ◎ ◎

"This," Lady Galatea said, "is where I live—and where you shall stay."

Allie stepped into the room and looked around. It was a stone-walled room with rough, bare ceiling beams. The windows were covered with oiled goatskin parchment, making the light that streamed into the room yellow and splotchy.

A blackened fireplace protruded into the room. There was no rug on the floor—just a thin scattering of straw. A bed made of dark wood stood in the middle of the floor, covered with a blanket of scratchy-looking black wool. A rough wooden table with a pewter washbasin stood in one corner, along with two wooden chairs. To Allie, the room looked about as comfortable as a prison cell.

"I shouldn't say this," Allie said, "but this place is depressing."

"This room is like my life," Lady Galatea said. "Life is harsh and full of sadness."

"Life can be wonderful," Allie said, "if you live it with faith and an open heart."

The lady smiled faintly. "Faith in what?" she asked. "Faith in God? Someday, Allie, you'll learn that faith is an illusion, God is a myth, and life is a road that leads nowhere."

"Has your life hurt you that much?" Allie asked.

"We will talk no more about my life," the lady answered. She looked Allie up and down with a grimace of disapproval. "Tell me—is that how ladies dress in the future?"

Allie looked at her overalls and white designer tee shirt. "Well—this is kind of casual. If I'd known I was going to meet a king today, I would have dressed up."

"I'm sure." The lady nodded. "And is it customary in your time for ladies to wear jewelry on their teeth?"

"Huh?" Allie put her hand to her mouth. "Oh! That's not jewelry—it's my braces—my 'tin grin.' The orthodontist gave me this metal mouth to make my teeth straight."

"The ortho—"

"The orthodontist," Allie said. "A type of tooth doctor. I know you don't have orthodontists in the Middle Ages, but I hope you at least have toothbrushes. I'll go nuts if I can't brush three times a day."

"A toothbrush?" Lady Galatea said. "I'll see what can be arranged."

Doctor Delyrius took Max to the laboratory table. "Do you know what these utensils are, lad?"

"Sure, most of them," Max said, picking up various pieces of equipment and looking them over. "I've got some of these in my chemistry set back home. You know—beakers, flasks, retorts, stuff like that."

"Ah," the Doctor said. "So the science of alchemy continues to be practiced in your century."

"Alchemy?" Max shook his head. "No. Chemistry, sure—but not alchemy. Nobody believes in alchemy anymore. In my time, everybody knows that alchemy is bogus."

Doctor Delyrius frowned. "Bogus?"

"That means fraud, fake, phony, a lie," Max said. He turned and squinted at some of the powders and liquids the Doctor kept on a wall shelf. There were also preserved dead animals in bottles of blown glass. Some of the creatures were dried and others were preserved in alcohol.

The Doctor scowled. "What are you saying, lad?"

"Well," Max said, "you alchemists want to turn lead into gold, right? And you're always looking for that whatchamadiggy that would let you live forever—the philosopher's stone."

"Yes," Doctor Delyrius said. "Of course."

"But that's bogus!" Max said. "You can't turn lead into gold, and there's no such thing as a philosopher's stone! You probably believe in astrology, right?"

"Certainly I believe in astrology," the Doctor said. "It's an established fact of science that the movements of the stars and planets foretell our destiny."

Max shook his head. "In my world," he said, "thinking people know that astrology is a scam."

"A scam?"

"Yeah," Max said. "A ripoff, a swindle, a fake."

Delyrius leaned toward Max. "You mean to say," he said, "that a thousand years from now, belief in astrology will cease to exist?"

"Oh, some people still believe in astrology," Max said. "In fact, just before I came through the Doorway, I was talking to a girl who is *really* into the zodiac and moon charts and all that stuff. But it's all a big fraud! In the twenty-first century, the only ones who believe in astrology are people who read supermarket tabloids and think Elvis lives in a UFO."

Doctor Delyrius looked completely mystified. "Elvis? UFO?"

"I'll give you another example of some of the bogus stuff you believe in," Max said. "You think that the universe is made of four elements, right? Air, earth, fire, and water?"

"Of course," the alchemist said. "This has been a law of science since the Greek philosopher Empedocles—"

"That's totally wrong!" Max said. "In the twenty-first century, we know that there aren't just four elements, there are a hundred and nine named elements, plus some that don't even have names yet. There's hydrogen, helium, lithium, beryllium—"

"Silence!" Delyrius roared, slamming his fist on the laboratory table. Glassware clattered and fell over.

Max shut his mouth.

"Do you realize what you're saying, lad?" the Doctor asked.

"I'm only trying to help you," Max said.

"Help me!"

"I thought you'd want to know the truth."

"Oh, the *truth!*" the Doctor said with thick sarcasm. "And what is this 'truth' you want me to know, lad? That everything I believe in is . . . as you say . . . bogus? That everything I have devoted my entire life to—my alchemy, my astrology—is nothing but a lie? Is that the 'truth' you want me to know?"

"Well, if you don't believe me—," Max began.

"The problem," the Doctor said, "is that I *do* believe you."

Max was surprised. "You do?"

"I spent all of last night studying that book," the Doctor said bitterly. He picked up *Rockets and Modern Warfare,* then tossed it back on the table. "In those pages, there is not one reference to alchemy, to the philosopher's stone, to any area of knowledge I have devoted my life to for all these years. So I do believe you, lad." Then, with a sarcastic sneer, he added, "Thank you for pointing out to me that my entire life has been wasted chasing fantasies."

"I'm sorry, Doctor," Max said. "I didn't want to make

you feel bad. I mean, it's not your fault you were born in an age of ignorance and superstition."

The Doctor turned his back on Max and threw his hands in the air. "He pities me! The boy is my prisoner! I hold the power of life and death over him! And still, he pities me!"

Max trembled. "I just—"

Doctor Delyrius whirled about, jabbing a bony finger in Max's face. "You will *not* pity me, understand? You will *fear* me!"

Max's eyes widened. He backed away. "Please, sir, I—"

"I want your answer, lad!" the Doctor demanded, stepping closer.

"My answer?" Max said. He backed into something. It was the Doorway.

"Will you help me build my rockets?" the Doctor roared in Max's face. "Or must your friends pay the price for your stubbornness?"

"I don't know!" Max said. "I—I need time to think!"

Doctor Delyrius stared strangely at Max for several seconds. Then he turned his back. He was silent for a long time, and the longer the old man's silence lasted, the more frightened Max became.

Finally, Max could stand it no longer. "Doctor," he said, "are you okay?"

Without warning, the alchemist reached up to a wall shelf and swept it with his arm. Bottles and jars went flying. They shattered on the floor. Cadmia, nix alba, spiritua fumans, mercurius praecipitatus, cinnabar, and oil of vitriol mixed and mingled, hissed and bubbled.

"Doctor!" Max shouted. "What are you doing?"

The old man's arm swept the next shelf. Algaroth, wismuth, zaffre, lapis infernalis, slaked lime, natron, sal ammoniac, and brimstone ran together, fuming and smoking, burning a hole in the floor.

Max backed away from the fumes. "Doctor!" he called. "That stuff is poisonous! We'll choke to death!"

Doctor Delyrius whirled about. The hem of his robe dragged through the fuming chemicals. Tendrils of smoke poured from his sleeves. As thick gray clouds rose around him, the old man looked more like a crazed wizard than ever before.

"So you need time to think, do you?" he snarled, his eyes ablaze with madness. He grabbed a torchstick from the floor and plunged it into the furnace. The torch began to blaze. "I'll give you time to think!"

Delyrius grabbed Max's wrist and pulled him toward the laboratory door. He dragged Max out of the laboratory and forced him down the stone staircase—toward the darkness.

"Where are we going?" Max asked.

"To the Hole!" he roared.

6

DESCENT INTO DARKNESS

Doctor Delyrius took Max to the bottommost chamber of
the tower. Once there, he placed the torch in a bracket,
where it gave off a sputtery light and greasy smoke. He
shut and locked the iron door of the chamber—there
would be no escape for Max.

Then the Doctor went to the middle of the stone floor
and lifted a round iron lid that was hinged to the floor. By
the torchlight, Max saw the Hole. A wooden ladder led
down inside.

"Don't make me go down there," Max pleaded.

"Get in."

Max considered struggling or running—but what was
the use? He breathed a silent prayer then went to the edge
of the Hole and looked down. He couldn't see the bottom.
He got down on the ladder, then climbed to the bottom and

looked up. With one swift motion, the Doctor reached down and pulled up the ladder.

"No!" Max said, grabbing for the ladder—but it was gone.

The metal lid at the top of the Hole slammed shut. Then Max heard the sound of departing footsteps, the groan of iron hinges, the clang of an iron door—then silence.

Max held his hands up before his eyes, but he couldn't see them. The darkness was complete.

Night came.

Though Grady was exhausted from a hard day's work in the stables, he couldn't sleep. He lay on a thin mat on the cold barracks floor, listening to Sir Osbert's loud snoring—and to Toby's faint sobbing. Grady's coarse wool blanket did little to shut out the night chill.

He had spent the past hour praying—praying for Max, who had been taken away by Doctor Delyrius; for Allie, who had been led away by a severe-looking woman dressed in black; for Toby, who was on the mat right next to him; and for his mother. He prayed most for her. Since his father's recent death, Grady often found himself worried about his mother.

It wasn't just worry that kept Grady awake, or the cold, or Sir Osbert's snoring. There was also the smell. The knights' barracks were built right over the stables—and the stable smell drifted up through the floor. The knights' beds were wooden bunks stacked two high. All the squires slept crowded on thin mats.

Grady was shivering, scared, and miserable—but he figured he wasn't as miserable as Toby. Grady raised his head and peered into the gloom. He could make out a dark, huddled mass shivering on the mat next to his.

"Hey, Toby!" Grady whispered.

Toby's faint sobbing abruptly stopped.

"Toby!" Grady whispered again. "Are you awake?"

"What do you want?"

"I can't sleep," Grady said. "I thought maybe you'd want to talk."

"What makes you think I want to talk?"

"Hey, if you want to go back to sleep—"

"No, no!" Toby said quickly. "I mean, if you want to talk, go ahead and talk. Dude, you already woke me up. What do you want to talk about?"

"I was wondering if you're, like, scared."

Toby was silent for several seconds. "Well, duh!" he said at last. "Aren't you?"

"Sure," Grady said. "But I've been praying and—"

"Stubblefield?"

"Yeah, Toby?"

"Spare me the Sunday school lesson, okay?"

"Whatever you say," Grady said. "You want to talk about home?"

"*My* home? What, are you, like, trying to depress me?"

"What do you mean?" Grady asked.

"Dude!" Toby whispered. "My old man's on the road most of the time. When he *does* comes home, he gets drunk and smacks me around. Then there's my mom, telling me what a no-good, worthless creep I am. Okay, we've talked about my home. Next subject."

"Well, we could talk about school."

"Oh, yeah!" Toby said. "You know what school is like for me? I come to school, and the jocks bodycheck me into the lockers and the preppies call me a fat loser. I go in the lunchroom and I've got no one to sit with because everybody hates me. Okay, we've talked about school."

"I didn't know," Grady whispered.

"You think I'm a real jerk, don't you? Always getting into fights and making life miserable for everybody."

"Well—," Grady said.

"I'll tell you something, Stubblefield," Toby said. "Even a jerk has his reasons. I know people are never going to like me. I don't have any friends and I never will. Okay, fine. I don't need friends. I don't care if people like me—as long as they're scared of me."

"Look, Toby," Grady said, "why don't we make a deal?"

"Huh?" Toby said. "What kind of deal?"

"Just for now, until we get out of this mess," Grady said, "why don't you and I look out for each other? You know, like . . . friends?"

"You and me? Friends?"

"Sure. Why not?" Grady said.

"I'll think about it."

Grady wasn't sure if Toby was being serious or sarcastic. But he did know that being cold, scared, and miserable can sometimes change a person. But Toby—change? Okay, not very likely. But who knows?

Lady Galatea pulled some blankets from under the bed and laid them out as a pallet on the wooden floor. The only light in the darkened room was the glow of a single candle by the lady's bedside.

"I'm sorry I have no proper bed to offer you, Allie," she said.

"I'll be fine on the floor," Allie said, kneeling and smoothing out the blankets. "We used to do a lot of camping before my parents' divorce, so I'm used to roughing it in a sleeping bag."

"'Roughing it'?" the lady asked.

"That means doing without the comforts of home. Roughing it is, like, sleeping on the floor or doing without pizza."

"Pizza?" the lady asked.

"Oh, that's right!" Allie said. "You've never had pizza! You'd love it. It's a food you don't have to make. You just phone out for it." Allie made a phone sign with her thumb and little finger, and put it to her ear. "You pick up the phone and tell the pizza people what kind you want. You know, pepperoni or sausage or—yuck!—anchovies."

"Phone?" asked the lady. "What is a phone?"

"It's a thingy that you talk into," said Allie, "and it carries your voice by wires, so you can have a conversation with people who are miles and miles away. Like, you can call the pizza parlor on the phone, place your order, and in half an hour, they bring the pizza right to your door."

"I'm afraid the supper I served you was a poor substitute for this . . . pizza," Lady Galatea said.

"Oh, the supper wasn't so bad," Allie said, trying to be as positive as she could. "You served bread and cheese, and that's what pizza's basically made out of." What Allie didn't mention was that the bread had been dry and tough, and the goat cheese had been vile and stinky.

Even though the food was terrible, Allie had enjoyed their supper together. The lady had asked question after question. She seemed endlessly fascinated by all the wonders of the twenty-first century—wonders that Allie simply took for granted.

After supper, Lady Galatea had given Allie the Middle Ages version of a toothbrush—a short stick that had been beaten and softened at one end to make it fibery and fringed. With a little water from a basin, she was able to do a decent job on her front teeth, though brushing her back molars had been almost impossible. The lady had even given Allie some mint leaves and sage to chew on—the Middle Ages version of breath mints. Even so, Allie still had the gross aftertaste of that goat cheese in her mouth.

"Your world is so full of wonders," Lady Galatea said, sitting on her own bed. "Machines that carry people through the air! Pictures that move and talk! And this Internet you speak of—I can't imagine how it works or what it is, but it sounds wonderful."

"Maybe I shouldn't talk so much," Allie said. She smoothed out the blankets, then lay down.

"Oh, but I enjoyed it," the lady said. "Though some things you've told me are hard to believe. . . . You're quite certain that the world is round? And that people live on the other side?"

"Oh, yeah!" Allie said. "That's where I came from—the other side of the world, a place called 'America.'"

"America," Lady Galatea said. She let the word melt on her tongue as if it were something sweet. "What a wondrous land it must be."

"Oh, it is," Allie said. "I just hope I can get back to it."

The lady's smile faded. "You must give up that hope, Allie," she said. "Castle Serpenfane is your home now."

"I can't give up hope," Allie said. "I mean, seeing a real castle and meeting a real king is awesome—even if the king is really nasty. But I believe God brought my friends and me here for a reason. When it's all over, He's going to take us back to our own time."

"I hope you're right," the lady said, "but in a way, I hope you're wrong."

"Wrong?" Allie said, her braces glistening in the candlelight. "Why?"

"Because," the lady said, "these few hours we've spent have been the first happy hours I've known in a long time."

"Were you ever happy?" Allie asked.

The lady smiled faintly, and a little sadly. "Yes, once," she said, gazing off as if she could see deep into the past. "Once I was very happy. I didn't always live here in a dark room at the top of a castle tower. When my husband lived, we had a wonderful life. I had servants and ladies-in-waiting and beautiful clothes to wear."

"What happened to your husband?" Allie said, then she added quickly, "If you don't mind my asking."

"Perhaps I shall tell you," said Lady Galatea. "But another time, not tonight."

"Okay," Allie said, crawling under her covers. "Good night."

The lady blew out the candle and settled into her bed. A few seconds passed.

"Allie," the lady called into the darkness. "Did you speak to me?"

"I'm sorry I bothered you," Allie said. "I was praying."

"Oh," the lady said. "I thought you spoke my name."

"I did," Allie said. "I was praying for you. I hope you don't mind."

"I don't mind," the lady said. "Good night, Allie."
"Good night, milady."

Max couldn't tell how much time had passed in the dark. He sat on the cold floor of the Hole, his back against the stone wall, drifting in and out of sleep.

His tee shirt and jeans didn't offer much warmth, and his skin felt as cold as stone and as bumpy as gooseflesh. If he let his imagination stray, he pictured creeping, crawling, slithering things all around him in the darkness. To take his mind off such thoughts, Max sang and thought up ideas for inventions. And then he prayed.

At first, Max half expected an angel to come save him from the darkness. An angel named Gavriyel had come to his rescue once during his previous adventure, when everything seemed dark and hopeless. But when several hours had passed in the darkened Hole, and no angel came, Max concluded that there would be no angels in *this* adventure.

He drifted into a fitful sleep—then awoke when something crawled over his hand. He flung the creature off in the inky darkness. It struck the stone wall with a *clack!* sound. Max figured it must have been some kind of beetle. Of course, a scorpion might make the same sound—but Max refused to consider *that* possibility.

Sometime later, he was awakened by the noise of his own wheezing. It sounded like wind whistling through a harmonica. He pulled out his inhaler and took a puff.

He thought about his friends, Allie and Grady, and wondered what they were doing. It was a comfort knowing that, wherever they were, they were thinking of him and praying for him.

He drifted off to sleep again. . . .

"Max."

The voice spoke so softly, he didn't even notice it at first. Had he imagined it?

"Max, I'm here with you. Don't be afraid."

Max heard it clearly. He recognized the voice. "I'm not scared," he said. "I was kind of hoping you'd come."

"I'm sorry I couldn't come sooner, but there are many hurting people in the world. They keep me very busy."

Max nodded. "It's okay. I prayed, and I wasn't alone."

"That's right, Max," the voice said. "You've never been alone."

"Are Grady and Allie okay?"

"I knew you'd ask, Max," the voice said, "so I checked on them before I came. Yes, they're fine."

"And Toby?"

"Well," the voice said, "you know Toby. He's still a problem. But I know you've been praying for him. The One who hears is pleased with your prayers. He wants you to know that He won't leave you in this pit."

"I knew He wouldn't," Max said.

"You're tired and cold. Would you like to sleep now?"

"Yeah," Max said. "I sure would."

Max noticed a faint golden glimmer in the darkness. The golden light grew, and as it grew, Max felt warmed. The warmth started at his skin and seeped into him, deeper and deeper, into his flesh, into his heart, into his soul. He yawned and closed his eyes. He could feel a nice, comfortable drowsiness come over him.

He started to doze—then he had a groggy moment of doubt, a fuzzy sense of unease. He wondered, *Am I really here? Or is it just a dream?*

Max opened his eyes. The golden glow was very bright. It was all around him, and there were no shadows anywhere. For a moment, Max was surprised. The light was so bright, it should have hurt his eyes—but it only made him feel warm and sleepy.

"Don't worry, Max," the voice said soothingly. "It's not a dream. And I'll stay with you while you sleep."

"Okay," Max said. "Thanks. . . . Oh, and Gavriyel?"

"Yes, Max?"

"There was a bug. It crawled on my hand."

"I sent it away. It won't bother you again."

Max nodded. "G'night."

"Good night, Max."

Hours passed. Max slept soundly. Toward morning, the glow slowly faded, and the cold crept near again.

7

A CLASH OF SWORDS

Grady swung his "sword" with all his might.

It was actually a blunt wooden practice sword called a waster. The wooden blade was cushioned with woolen padding—and so was Grady. His body and limbs were clad in thick practice padding, and his head was enclosed in a cagelike helmet of metal bars.

Grady's waster hit his opponent's waster with a muffled *thwock!* and knocked it aside. His opponent was a boy named Piers—older and taller than Grady, but thinner, with gaunt cheeks, intensely blue eyes, and a thatch of straw-colored hair. Piers retreated from Grady's attack, raising his waster.

It was early morning, and the two boys battled each other in the castle courtyard, surrounded by twenty other boys and several knights. The boys, all of them squires, were yelling, cheering, and calling out encouragement to Piers. He was their hero—the best swordfighter of them all.

Toby was there, too, cheering and yelling, eager to get his turn. Whacking at guys with wooden swords looked like fun—maybe the only kind of fun a guy could have in the Middle Ages.

Grady advanced and swung—*thwock!* Piers retreated another step. Grinning and confident, Grady charged the blond-haired boy, whacking and slashing with abandon, intent on landing a blow against Piers's padded ribs.

Then Piers surprised Grady.

Instead of retreating, he stepped forward and to his left, close to Grady but sidestepping the full fury of Grady's wild attack. From a classic swordsman's position called the "prima" stance, Piers cut diagonally upward to the right, knocking Grady's sword aside. Then, once Grady's body was exposed to his waster, Piers attacked with two downward-slashing blows called "hawks." The blows caught Grady square in the chest. Despite his thick padding, the force surprised Grady, driving him backward.

Now on the defensive, Grady brought his waster up to defend himself—but his attempt to cover his chest only exposed his ribs to Piers's swift, expertly delivered hawk-blows. Grady staggered, lost his footing, and fell to the grass. His waster went flying from his grasp.

Rising to his knees, Grady lunged for his fallen weapon—

Thunk! A huge black boot landed on the blade. Grady looked up and saw Sir Guy towering over him.

"Enough!" Sir Guy snapped. "The battle is over." He removed his boot from Grady's waster, walked over to the blond squire, and raised Piers's sword hand in the air. "Hail the victor!"

The squires cheered.

Grady stood and removed the practice helmet, setting it in the grass beside the wooden practice sword. Then he grinned and offered his hand to Piers. The blond squire took Grady's hand with a strong grip.

"You have strength and boldness," Piers said. "With practice, you'll make a fine swordsman." He grinned, then added, "Though not as good as I am, of course."

Max's eyes came slowly open. For a moment, he was disoriented. He couldn't understand why he saw total darkness with his eyes wide open. Then he remembered he was in the Hole, and there was no light at all in the Hole.

And yet—

The last he remembered, there had been *a lot* of light—golden light that warmed him inside and out. The outer warmth was gone now, but the inner warmth was still there, deep inside him.

He heard groaning iron hinges and approaching footsteps.

The lid over the Hole made a scraping sound as it was pried open.

"Max," said a voice from above. This voice was cold and dreadful—but Max wasn't afraid.

"Yes, Doctor?" Max answered.

There was a long silence. Finally, the voice said, "Is that all you have to say, boy? I've seen grown men beg to be let out of the Hole. You sit there in the darkness as if you enjoy it."

"It's no fun," Max said. "But I haven't been lonely."

From above came only stunned silence. Max waited.

"Doctor?" he said at last. "Can I get out of here now?"

Again, there was no answer. But a few moments later, a ladder was lowered into the Hole.

Henry the Lesser was the shortest of the squires. He was as skinny as a rake handle, with long brown hair and big ears that stuck out like clamshells. He was called Henry the Lesser to distinguish him from another squire named Henry who was sixty pounds heavier and a head taller.

As Grady and Piers were talking, Henry the Lesser walked up to Grady and touched his arm.

"What are you doing, runt?" Piers asked, scowling at the smaller boy.

"His skin is so dark!" Henry the Lesser said. "I've never seen anyone with dark skin before!"

"Well, let him be," Piers said.

"It's okay," Grady said. "He's not bothering me."

"What do they call people like you?" Henry the Lesser asked. "People with dark skin, I mean?"

"I'm an African-American," Grady said.

"African-American," Henry the Lesser said slowly. "Hmm. Well, what about the other boy? What do you call him?" He pointed to Toby.

A short distance away, Sir Osbert was helping Toby into his padding and helmet, getting him ready for his first swordfight.

Grady shrugged. "I guess you'd say he's a white American."

"He sure is white," Henry the Lesser said. "His skin is as white as a fish belly."

"There you go, lad," Sir Osbert said, putting a wooden practice sword in Toby's hand. "You're ready for battle."

"Dude!" shouted Toby, waving his waster. "Who wants to fight me? Bring 'em on!"

"I'll match swords with you—dude!" Henry the Lesser shouted.

Grady blinked in surprise. "Did you say—?"

But Henry the Lesser was already rushing over to Sir Osbert to be suited up for battle.

Reynard, a thickset, brown-haired squire, turned to Piers. "That word 'dude,'" he said. "What do you suppose it means?"

"I think," Piers said, "that it is something like when we say, 'Hail fellow well met.' Am I correct, Grady?"

Grady nodded. "Yeah . . . something like that," he said.

Allie and Lady Galatea walked out through the front gate of the castle, across the drawbridge, and over the wide moat. They turned off the dusty road that led to the village and headed across a green meadow toward the woods.

The lady was dressed in a loose-fitting black tunic, black breeches, and boots of supple leather. Her long black hair was bound by a ribbon of red silk. The lady also had found new clothes for Allie to wear—a boy's green tunic and brown breeches. She offered Allie a pair of deerskin shoes, but Allie decided to keep her white-and-gray Nike tennis shoes, instead.

At the edge of the woods, Allie paused to look back at Castle Serpenfane. It stood gray and majestic, its stone towers and spires rising skyward above the notched battlements of its grim, gray walls. "I still can hardly believe I'm here," she said, "in a world of castles and knights."

"How odd," Lady Galatea said. "You tell me you come from a world of wonders I can scarcely imagine. Chariots without horses—what did you call them? Cars! And these Michael-wave machines that cook your meals—"

"You mean microwave ovens?"

"Ah, *micro*wave, is it? I thought this wonderful invention was named after Michael the Archangel. There are so many wonders in your world—yet it is my simple world that fascinates you."

"Well," Allie said, "if I ever get back to my own century, I'll never take it for granted again."

"Come along," the lady said. "The place we're going is not much farther."

Toby came at Henry the Lesser, sword whirling like a propeller. Henry laughed, easily fending the blows. Toby swung so wildly, he tripped over his sword and landed on his face.

"Get up and keep fighting!" Sir Osbert shouted. "He hasn't stuck you yet. You've only tripped over your own feet!"

The crowd of squires laughed.

Toby jumped up and dashed after Henry the Lesser. *Thunk-thwack-thock!* Their blades collided in a rapid-fire rhythm. Then, as Toby was aiming his best shot at the smaller boy's ribs—*swish!* His blade hit nothing but air. Henry the Lesser danced away, chuckling.

"Come back here, you wuss!" Toby shouted.

"Have at you, prattling knave!" Henry the Lesser shouted, stepping quickly toward Toby.

"Huh?" Toby said.

Henry the Lesser delivered a punishing hawk-blow to Toby's padded ribs. Toby's waster flew out of his hand and he tumbled onto his back. "Okay, okay, you win! I'm killed!" he said, putting out his hand. "Help me up!"

Henry the Lesser took off his helmet and stretched out his hand. Toby took the boy's hand—then scissored Henry's ankle with his legs and pulled him off balance. Henry the Lesser tumbled onto the grass next to Toby.

To Toby's surprise, the boy was *laughing*. Toby thought he was getting even with Henry the Lesser—but the boy thought it was funny.

"A merry jest, dude!" The smallest squire laughed. "A merry jest, indeed!"

@ @ @

"Galatea is a beautiful name," Allie said as they walked through the cool woods. "I've never heard it before."

"My name comes from the tales of the ancient Greeks," the lady said. "My mother loved the old myths, and she named me Galatea after a beautiful mermaid in an old story."

They reached the end of the wood and there it was: a sunny green meadow, level and grassy. The lady unbuckled her sword and hung it on a tree bough.

"It's beautiful here," Allie said. "Let's run!"

"All right," the lady said. "But gently, just enough to limber our legs."

Allie bent down and touched her toes a few times to stretch her calf muscles. Then the lady and Allie took off at an easy pace across the meadow.

When they came back, the lady was surprised. "Why, Allie, you aren't even breathing hard."

"I play a lot of soccer," Allie said.

"Very well, then," the lady said. "Let us begin your training." She went to the tree, retrieved her sword belt, and buckled it on. Then she drew the sword, and it flashed in the sunlight. It had a narrow blade and a keen edge.

"Cool!" Allie said, her eyes wide.

"It's Persian watered steel," the lady said.

"Watered steel?" Allie asked.

"It is so called because of these waterlike markings," Galatea said.

Allie looked closely and saw fine, wavy bands of dark and light metal in the surface of the blade. "It's a beautiful sword," Allie said. "It's a shame that something so beautiful is used to cause pain and death."

Lady Galatea stiffened. "I will overlook that," she said sternly.

She turned and walked out into the meadow. Facing Allie, she held the sword out before her. "Now, the sword strikes in seven ways," she said. "Two cuts downward." She slashed diagonally to the right, then left. "Two cuts across." She slashed horizontally right, then left. "Two cuts upward." Right, left. "And the thrust." She placed her left hand against the ball-shaped pommel at the base of the sword, and shoved the sword forward.

Allie pictured those moves being used against a human opponent—and she shuddered.

"Now, watch closely," Lady Galatea said.

"No," Allie said. "I can't." She turned her back on the lady.

"Face me!" Galatea said sternly.

"I could never use a sword," Allie said over her shoulder.

"Of course you could, Allie," the lady replied. "It's not heavy—"

"No," Allie said, turning around. "I mean I could never use a sword to hurt another person. And I wouldn't lift a finger, much less a sword, to serve King Wyvern and the Silver Dragon."

Lady Galatea put her blade back in its scabbard and walked toward Allie, a look of displeasure on her face. "I have accepted you as my apprentice," she said. "If you do not do as I say—"

"Do you know how to fall, milady?" Allie interrupted.

Galatea looked at her in surprise. "I beg your pardon?"

"You've never learned how to fall, have you?" Allie asked.

"One does not *learn* to fall," the lady said curtly.

"Oh, yes, one does!" Allie said. "There's a right way to fall—and a lot of wrong ways. I found that out when I started taking karate."

"Taking what?"

"Karate," Allie said. "It's self-defense training. I'm not real good at it yet, but I've been taking lessons for two years. When I started, my instructor said I had to learn how to fall before I could learn anything else."

"I fail to see—"

"I wanted to learn how to do karate kicks and hit with the side of my hand and block the other guy and all that karate stuff," Allie said, demonstrating a kick, a chop, and a block.

Startled by Allie's moves, the lady backed away.

"But," Allie said, "my instructor said I could really hurt myself unless I learned how to fall the right way."

"Allie—"

"The thing is, I was scared to fall—so I refused to learn how. Finally, my instructor did *this* to me—" Allie put out her leg, grabbed the lady's arm, and dropped her onto the grass.

Galatea looked up at Allie with startled eyes. "How did you—"

"I looked up at him," Allie said, "the same way you're looking at me."

The lady got to her feet and kept a cautious distance from Allie.

"So," Allie said, "I decided I'd better learn how to fall— and I did, see?" She turned and ran toward the meadow, leaped, tucked her body, did a shoulder roll, and immediately whirled back onto her feet.

Lady Galatea looked at Allie with her mouth open. "How did you do that?"

"It's easy—see?" Allie did three more rolls in quick succession. "You just have to know how to fall."

"Could—" The lady hesitated. "Could you teach me how to fall like that?"

"Sure I could," Allie said.

"It could be a useful skill," the lady said, "especially in battle. If you were knocked down or unhorsed, you could simply tumble and come right back to your feet."

"Exactly," Allie said. "And knowing how to fall can be a useful skill in life, too."

The lady's eyes narrowed. "What do you mean?"

"My karate teacher once told me," Allie said, "that the skills you learn in karate are just like the skills you need in life. Sometimes life knocks you down, and you have to know how to fall safely, so you can get back up and keep going."

"Ah, I see now," Lady Galatea said stiffly, a flush rising to her cheeks. "You, a mere schoolgirl, have decided to instruct me in how to live my life."

"Please don't be angry, milady," Allie said. "It's just that—well, I think you got knocked down sometime in your life, and something got broken inside you—something in your soul. If only you would—"

"Allie," the lady said coldly, "you are meddling in matters you do not understand." And without another word, Lady Galatea turned and walked back through the woods.

Allie shook her head. *I tried to help her,* she thought, *but it looks like I just made a mess of things.* With a sigh, she followed the lady back toward the castle.

8

IT'S ONLY ROCKET SCIENCE

Torch in hand, Doctor Delyrius led Max up the spiral staircase of the tower and into the darkened laboratory. "Sit over there, lad," the Doctor said.

Max walked over to the three-legged stool and sat down. There was a harsh chemical smell in the room. Max wondered what time it was. He knew it was daytime, but whether morning, noon, or afternoon, he couldn't say.

"Sir," Max said, "I'm kind of hungry and thirsty. I haven't eaten since—"

"All right, all right," the Doctor said impatiently. He grabbed a cloth-wrapped object from a shelf and tossed it to Max. "There! Eat your fill!"

"Thank you," Max said, catching it. He opened the cloth and found a loaf of bread, about a third of which was hidden by blotches of dark green mold. Max broke a piece off the unmoldy end. The bread was as hard, dry, and crumbly as soda crackers. It didn't matter—Max was hungry.

"Drink this," said the Doctor, slamming a clay pot in front of Max.

Max looked at the pot. A dead fly floated on the water. The bread and the water had obviously been sitting on the laboratory shelf for a long time. Max dipped two fingers into the pot and flicked the fly out of the water, then took a drink.

As he ate and drank, Max looked around. He couldn't make out much detail in the gloom-wrapped chamber—just the great hulking furnace against one wall, the big laboratory table in the middle of the room, and the faint gleam of the golden Doorway—its gilded surfaces and quartz crystals managed to catch the few stray rays of sunlight that filtered in around the shutters.

Without warning, Doctor Delyrius unshuttered a window. Brilliant white sunlight exploded into the room, etching every detail of the laboratory with an eye-piercing glare. Max squinted and shielded his eyes.

Then he got his first good look at Doctor Delyrius since he had been in the Hole. The Doctor's cloak and robes were stained, burned, and eaten around the edges by acids. The wrinkles and crags of the Doctor's face had deepened, giving his face a monstrous appearance. His left eye twitched. His bony hands were so waxy and pale that the sunlight passed through them like x-rays.

Max glanced at the floor. There was an ugly splotch

there—charred in some places, bleached white in others, and stained gray or vile green in others. Someone had swept away the debris and broken bottles, but the acids and poisons had left a mark that could not be removed from the oak floor.

"What are you looking at, boy?" the Doctor growled.

Max snapped to attention. "Nothing, sir," he said.

The Doctor pulled something out of the depths of his robes and slammed it on the table. It was the book from Max's father's study, *Rockets and Modern Warfare*.

"You've had the night to think," the Doctor said. "Now, what is your answer? Will you help me?"

"I—," Max hesitated. Again he silently prayed to God for wisdom and guidance before giving his answer.

"Yes, boy?" the Doctor said. "And remember that the fate of your friends hangs on your answer."

Max looked at the floor and muttered something.

"What's that?" Doctor Delyrius said. "Speak up, boy."

Max looked up and met the old man's eye. "I said I'll help you."

The Doctor's face relaxed. "Excellent!" he said. "We shall begin at once."

Max and Doctor Delyrius talked and worked through the afternoon and long into the night. Using a stick of charcoal and a sheet of lambskin vellum, Max sketched as he talked. "The people in China were the first to develop rockets," he explained. "They called them 'fire arrows.'"

"China?" Doctor Delyrius asked.

"Yeah," Max said. "Only I think China was called Cathay back in the Middle Ages."

"Oh, yes," the Doctor said. "Cathay, in the Far East."

"I guess so," Max said, scratching his head. "I'm not very good at geography. About two hundred years from now, a guy named Marco Polo will go from Italy to China. I'm not sure, but I think that's why chow mein noodles and spaghetti are so much alike."

"Let us confine our thoughts to rockets, shall we?" the Doctor said.

Max shrugged, and continued sketching on the vellum sheet. "Remember the space shuttle I told you about? The solid rocket boosters on the space shuttle use basically the same technology as the Chinese fire arrows. You just load a big tube with fuel, ignite it, and *whoosh!* It takes off and keeps going till all the fuel is burned up."

"What are these fire arrows made of?" the Doctor asked.

"Bamboo," Max said. "Whoa, that's a problem! Bamboo doesn't grow around here."

"What is bamboo?"

"A plant—a type of grass, actually—kind of like a tree, but hollow inside," Max explained.

Doctor Delyrius studied Max's drawing for a moment—then he took the charcoal from Max's hand and made a drawing of his own. It looked something like a wooden barrel or wine cask—only it was long and cigar-shaped instead of short, fat, and barrel-shaped.

"It could work!" the Doctor said. "I'll show this drawing to the cooper. He just might be able to build rocket bodies out of barrel staves."

"What's a cooper?" Max asked. "And what are barrel staves?"

"A cooper is a maker of barrels," the Doctor said. "And staves are the wooden pieces a barrel is made of."

Unfortunately, the Doctor's idea sounded workable.

"Well," Doctor Delyrius said excitedly, "we're making excellent progress! Now we need a warhead!"

"Warhead?"

"Yes! The book said that a rocket weapon must have a warhead—a large mass of explosives at the top of the rocket. It must have a large, powerful warhead capable of destroying castle walls and killing many knights."

Max's heart sank. His plan wasn't working out the way he thought it would. The Doctor's scientific knowledge may have been primitive compared with twenty-first-century science, but the man was no fool. Max had been trying to give the Doctor partial, incomplete, and even misleading information—but the Doctor was smart enough to fill in the gaps, like quickly coming up with a substitute for bamboo.

Max yawned. He was tired and discouraged—and he was beginning to think he had made the wrong decision by agreeing to help Doctor Delyrius. He had prayed and asked God for wisdom—but everything Max did seemed to turn out all wrong.

Had God let him down?

Allie knelt on the straw-strewn floor and smoothed out the heavy woolen blankets of her pallet. A few feet away, Lady Galatea turned down her bed and prepared to retire for the night. She was about to blow out the candle when Allie interrupted.

"Lady Galatea," Allie asked, "what happened here?"

The lady turned and gave Allie a questioning look. "What do you mean?"

"I've read about the Middle Ages," Allie said. "I'm no expert, but I know something about chivalry and knights. I know that the people of the Middle Ages didn't worship a Silver Dragon. They prayed to the one true God. Every morning, the lord of the castle and all the people would go to the chapel to worship and pray, and then they would go on about their work."

"That's true," the lady said, sitting on the edge of the bed. "That is how it once was in this castle—before King Wyvern."

"Tell me about it," Allie said. "Tell me what life was like when this was a Christian castle."

"Oh, Allie," the lady said, "it's so late, and—"

"Please," Allie said.

The lady considered. "Very well," she said at last. "Before Wyvern became king, this castle had another name. For four hundred years, it was called Castle Mageste—named in honor of the majesty of God. The last Christian ruler was King Vyncent. The kingdom was called Gracea then."

"Gracea," Allie said. "Then why was the name changed to Gyle?"

"King Wyvern changed the name of the kingdom from Gracea to Gyle when he took power."

"What kind of man was King Vyncent?" Allie asked.

"He was a humble man—honest, just, and faithful to his God. Vyncent ruled wisely, and the Kingdom of Gracea was happy and at peace. There was not much silver and gold in the kingdom in those days. But the people had enough to eat, a roof over their heads, clothes to wear, and honest work to do. No one was greedy for gold in those days. Even King Vyncent's simple crown was made of iron, not gold. But King Vyncent had a rival—"

"Wyvern?" Allie asked.

"Yes, his younger brother, Prince Wyvern. One day, King Vyncent was found dead in his bedchamber—and Wyvern became king. Some whispered that Vyncent had been poisoned, for King Wyvern had a friend—"

Allie gasped. "You mean Doctor Delyrius! He must have provided the poison that killed King Vyncent! An alchemist would know all about poisons!"

"I suppose," the lady said.

Allie frowned. "So King Wyvern shut down the chapel and—"

"Not right away," Lady Galatea said. "At first, King Wyvern allowed worship to continue in the chapel. He even went to the chapel himself and pretended to pray. But at the same time, he sent his armies abroad to conquer other kingdoms and plunder other castles for gold and silver. The Kingdom of Gyle was no longer happy and peaceful—but it was very rich. The poor saw their sons go to war and never return. But the noblemen supported the wars that lined their pockets with gold."

"Couldn't anyone stop King Wyvern?" Allie asked.

"Stop him?" the lady said. "How can you stop the king? The king's will is law."

"Even if he became the king by murdering his own brother?" Allie asked in a shocked voice.

"It doesn't matter how the king acquired his crown," Galatea said. "He is the king, and his will must be obeyed." She cupped her hand behind the candle to blow it out.

"Milady?" Allie said.

The lady paused. The candle still burned. "Yes, Allie?"

"Is there any way to get inside the chapel?" She paused. "I'd like to pray there."

"Oh?" the lady said. "And what would you pray for?"

"I would pray that this kingdom would be restored to what it once was," Allie said.

The lady seemed lost in thought. The candle's glow glimmered in her dark eyes.

"I guess it's impossible," Allie said with a sigh. "After all, the chapel is boarded up, and—"

"Actually," Lady Galatea said, "there is a way to get in." She glanced at Allie, and there was a mischievous gleam in

her eye. "What would you rather do tonight? Go to sleep—
or have a midnight adventure?"

It was Grady's second night in the barracks, breathing the
"barnyard perfume" from the stables while listening to Sir
Osbert's snoring. Grady pulled the blanket around him and
tried to get comfortable. No use. He was never going to
fall asleep while he was so uncomfortable. At least Toby
wasn't whimpering.

"Toby!" Grady whispered. "Hey, Toby!"

"Yeah?" Toby said.

"Did I wake you up?"

"Well, duh!" Toby hissed. "It's after midnight! What do
you want?"

"Remember what we were talking about last night?"

"Huh?" Toby paused. "What was that?"

"You were telling me how tough things are at home—"

A strange sound came from Toby's direction—as if he
was snorting through his nose.

"Toby?" Grady whispered.

The snorting turned to gasping.

"Are you okay?" Grady asked. It sounded like Toby was
either sobbing . . . or choking . . . or . . .

Toby stifled his laughter with his hand.

On the bunk, Sir Osbert snored louder and rolled over.

"What's so funny?" Grady asked.

"Dude, you bought it!" Toby snickered. "You really fell for it, man!" Then he began mocking his own words from the previous night. "'Oh, poor me! My old man's a drunk and everybody at school hates me and I don't have any friends! Boo-hoo!'" He switched to a Grady impression. "'There, there, Toby, I'll be your friend!' Dude, I strung you along, and you totally fell for it!"

Grady rolled over. *Try to be a friend,* he thought, *and this is what it gets you.* His face was hot with humiliation.

Then the thought came to him: *If Toby ever changes, it won't be quick or easy. But whether Toby changes or not, the important thing is that I did what is right.* Grady sensed that the thought came to him from God Himself. The moment he felt God speaking to him, Grady felt a warm sense of peace. In seconds, he was asleep.

On the mat next to Grady, Toby shivered long into the night—cold, scared, and alone.

9

THE MAZE AT MIDNIGHT

Allie could hardly contain her excitement. She and Lady Galatea were going to sneak into the chapel at midnight! The lady wouldn't explain how they would get into the chapel, which only made the entire late-night venture seem more mysterious and exciting. Allie knew that if she and Lady Galatea were caught in the forbidden chapel at midnight, the consequences would be harsh.

Allie looked over at the lady and saw her strapping a sword and scabbard over her black robe. Allie wondered why the lady wore a sword—but she didn't ask because she didn't want to know.

"We are taking a secret path to the chapel," the lady said, "and the way will be cold and dark." She handed Allie a folded cloak and a cloth bag with something heavy in it. "Put the cloak on and tie the bag to your belt. I'll get some torches."

Allie unfolded the cloak and put it on. It was hooded and black—it seemed as though Lady Galatea owned nothing that wasn't black. Allie shook the cloth bag, and it jingled. "A bag of coins?" she asked, tying the draw-cords of the bag to her belt. "What are these for?"

"You'll see," Galatea said.

The lady took two big sticks from a pile on the floor. The ends of the sticks were wrapped in strips of cloth dipped in beeswax. She tucked one into her sword belt and lit the other in the fireplace. "Let's go quickly," Galatea said. "Each of these torches lasts about half an hour. With two, we'll have an hour of torchlight, no more."

Allie followed the lady out of her chamber and down the spiral staircase, all the way to the dark cellar below the tower. The cellar was used for storage and was filled with oak barrels of cider and mead wine, sacks of grain and salt, clay pots of honey and oil, bolts of cloth, coils of rope, and other goods. As the torchlight penetrated the corners of the cellar, Allie heard tiny rodent feet scuttling in the shadows.

Lady Galatea placed the torch in an iron bracket in the wall. "Help me move these sacks," she said softly.

Allie and Galatea moved six sacks to clear a section of the floor. "There it is," the lady said. Allie looked and saw nothing but floorboards. The lady drew her sword and inserted the blade into a knothole. Using the sword for leverage, she pried at the board and a whole section lifted up—a hidden door! Allie helped Galatea pull back the door. There were stone steps leading down into a darkened subcellar.

Allie peered into the darkness. "We have to go down there?" she asked. Suddenly, she wasn't so sure she wanted to see the chapel *that* badly.

"Are you afraid?" Galatea asked.

"No," Allie said. Then she bit her lower lip. "Actually, yes. I see things crawling down there."

Galatea took the torch and held it in the hole. Glistening albino worms wriggled in the torchlight. They looked like wet, crawly fingers.

"*Eeeuww!*" Allie said, grimacing. "Totally gross!"

Galatea laughed. "Don't worry," she said. "They don't bite."

"I know," Allie said, wrapping the cloak tightly around herself. "But they *squish!*"

"Come along," the lady said. Holding the torch high, she started down the stone steps. When Galatea was all the way to the bottom, Allie still stood at the edge of the hole, working up her courage.

"Hurry!" the lady called. "These torches won't last forever!"

"Okay," Allie replied in a squeaky voice. She started down, placing her feet carefully on each step. Finally . . . *Squish!* "Eeeuww!" Allie squealed. *Squish!* "Sick!"

The stone floor was wet and slick, and coated here and there with black or gray fungus. The air was damp and smelled like rotting things. Rubble was strewn about—

chunks of porous white stone in various shapes and sizes. Water dripped from the cracked stone ceiling and made plinking sounds on the floor. The flickering torch in Galatea's hand cast weird, shifting shadows that seemed to hide dark, crawling things.

The lady lifted the hem of her robe with one hand to avoid dragging it in water, fungus, and worms. Allie cringed with every step, thinking of all the worm goosh that clogged the waffle soles of her Nikes.

Soon, they reached a stone wall. Some of the stones in the wall were smooth and white, others were dark. The ancient wall had once partly collapsed, then was later rebuilt with newer, darker stones. In the middle of the wall was a narrow opening.

"The maze begins through there," Galatea said.

"Maze!" Allie said, shocked and dismayed. "We have to go through a maze?"

"Don't worry," the lady said. "The maze is easy to follow—if you know the secret." She turned and slipped through the opening.

Allie followed and found herself in a place where the ceiling didn't drip and the paving stones were dry. She was relieved to find that there were no more worms underfoot. In front of her was a bewildering series of walls and openings.

The floor was made of limestone blocks in various shapes and sizes. "The castle above our heads was built on the ruins of an old Roman fortress," the lady explained. "These white stones were laid down by the Romans."

But Allie noticed newer, darker stones set in the floor. The dark stones formed pathways that branched in different directions, leading off into the various corridors and rooms of the maze.

Lady Galatea held the torch low, as if searching for something on the floor. "Here it is!" she said.

"What?" Allie said. "What did you find?"

"Dominus," Galatea said.

"What?" Allie said. Then she looked down and saw that the woman stood on a large dark stone with a single word carved onto its face: DOMINUS.

The lady began to walk, following a row of dark stones. With each step she chanted: "Pascit . . . me . . . nihil . . . mihi . . . deerit . . . in . . . *pascuis*."

Allie followed behind Galatea. The next six stones after the DOMINUS stone were blank. When she said the word "pascuis," she was standing on a stone marked PASCUIS. From the PASCUIS stone, the path of dark stones branched in four directions, leading to four different doorways.

"Allie," Galatea said, "open the bag and place a coin on that stone."

Baffled but obedient, Allie took a shiny coin from her bag and placed it on the PASCUIS stone.

"I think we go this way," Galatea said. She started walking, following the third path from the left. ". . . Herbarum . . . adclinavit . . . me . . . super . . . aquas . . . refectionis . . .

enutrivit . . . *me*." The stone under her feet was marked ME.

"Those words—," Allie said. "They're Latin, aren't they?" She placed a shiny coin on the ME stone. "You're reciting something in Latin, one word for each stone—and the words on the stones tell you if you're going the right way or not! That is so cool!"

Galatea didn't answer. She was focused on the words she chanted: "Animam . . . meam . . . refecit . . . duxit . . . me . . . per . . . semitas . . . iustitiae . . . propter . . . *nomen*." Standing on a stone in a doorway, she looked at her feet. The stone read VENIT. "No," she said, "this is the wrong way. It must be that way." She retraced her steps and took a different direction, arriving at a different doorway. The stone under her feet read NOMEN. She continued on.

The lady led Allie through the maze of corridors, doorways, and rooms. They had to backtrack several times, but the words carved in the paving stones kept them on the right path. After about ten minutes in the maze, the path opened into a cave or grotto. Galatea recited, ". . . habitabo . . . in . . . domo . . . Domini . . . in . . . longitudine . . . *dierum*." The last stone on the path was marked DIERUM. There were no more dark stones. They had reached the end of the maze.

"With those clues on the stones," Allie said, "the maze was easy."

"Yes," Lady Galatea said. "And without those clues, a

wanderer would soon be hopelessly lost. Imagine trying to feel your way through the maze in total darkness."

Allie shivered at the thought—then pushed it out of her mind. "The Latin words you recited—," Allie said. "They sounded beautiful, even though I didn't understand them. What do they mean in English?"

"'The Lord is my shepherd,'" Galatea quoted. "'Therefore I can lack nothing. He shall feed me in green pastures, and lead me beside the waters of comfort—'"

"Oh, the Twenty-third Psalm!" Allie said, her eyes sparkling in the torchlight. "I love those words! It's as if God was speaking to us, leading us through the maze— 'through the valley of the shadow of death.'"

"I memorized those words as a child," Galatea said, a faraway look in her eyes. "Then, the world was a simple place, and it was easy for me to believe. But I've been through the valley of the shadow of death, and I was all alone. The words of that psalm no longer mean anything to me. They are just clues to a maze. Let's move on."

The lady turned and walked on into the darkness of the cave. Allie sighed, whispered a prayer for the lady, and trudged along after her.

The floor of the cave sloped gently upward. By the torchlight, Allie observed regular shapes in the cave walls on both the right and the left. They almost seemed like cemetery headstones carved into the walls.

Allie gasped and stopped in her tracks.

Ahead of her, the lady halted and turned. "What's wrong?"

"There are *dead* people buried here!" Allie said.

"Of course," Galatea said. "We're in the chapel crypt. Come along."

Allie had no choice but to follow—or be left in total darkness among the dead. It's not that Allie was superstitious or believed in ghosts. But the idea of being underground and surrounded by dead people just seemed . . . creepy.

Lady Galatea paused before one of the graves and held the torch so Allie could read the inscription:

SIR ROWLAND of HURST
CHRISTIAN WARRIOR
NOW KNOWS PEACE IN HIS FATHER'S HOUSE

Passing the torch from her right hand to her left, the lady traced the sign of the cross with her right hand upon her forehead and chest. Her eyes glistened in the firelight.

"Why did you do that," Allie said, "if you don't believe in God?"

The lady answered simply, "Because he believed."

"Sir Rowland was your husband?" Allie asked.

"Yes," the lady said. "He was a good Christian knight— a man who lived by the Code of Knighthood."

"But how could he serve an evil king like Wyvern?" Allie asked.

"At first, remember, King Wyvern posed as a Christian," the lady said. "It was only after King Wyvern had solidified his power that he closed the chapel, tore down the cross, and put up the images of the Silver Dragon. By that time, my beloved Rowland was dead."

"Sir Rowland died in battle?" Allie asked.

"Yes, in one of the king's wars of conquest. He rode to war at the Battle of Old Chertsey Hill. I spent the next three days and nights in the chapel, on my knees, praying for his safe return. Finally, my husband's comrades brought him back to me on his shield, dead."

"I'm so sorry," Allie said. "But why do you blame God? Why don't you blame King Wyvern?"

The lady thought for a moment. "Allie, there's a great gulf between your world and mine," she said. "Your questions suggest that a king should answer to a higher law, as if he were a mere peasant. In my world, the king's will is the law. He answers to no one, and no one questions his will."

"But that is so messed up!" Allie said. "No king is above God's law—not even King David or any other great king in the Bible. And a king who would kill his own brother or start a bunch of wars just to get more gold—he's just an evil king who doesn't deserve to rule!"

There was an amused half-smile on the lady's face. "What a quaint notion." She turned and walked on.

Allie followed.

The lady paused once more, shining the torchlight on a large, imposing grave—a recessed niche containing a stone coffin, with two angel statues standing at the head and foot of the coffin. There was an inscription in large letters on the wall behind the coffin. The inscription read:

KING VYNCENT

SERVANT TO HIS LORD, SERVANT TO HIS PEOPLE

"UBI EST, MORS, VICTORIA TUA?

UBI EST, MORS, STIMULUS TUUS?"

"What do the Latin words mean?" Allie asked.

"'Where, O death, is your victory?'" the lady quoted. "'Where, O death, is your sting?'" The torch in her hand sputtered. "We must hurry to the chapel."

A few more steps brought them to a richly carved archway. Passing through the archway, they arrived in the chapel. It was the raised area called the chancel—the place where the priest would lead the worship service. In the rear of the chancel, three stained-glass windows rose toward a high vaulted ceiling.

On the chancel wall, Allie saw a painting depicting a knight in golden armor. The knight held his sword out with the hilt up and blade down, so that it resembled a cross. There was also a cross emblazoned upon his shield. Next to the knight were these words in large letters:

The Vow of Chivalry

I vow to be loyal to my God and my king;
To seek the fellowship of good men;
To live humbly and courteously before all;
To allow no reproach or offense to any lady;
To defend the Holy Faith;
To face battle with courage, and death with honor.

"Those were the words my husband lived by," Galatea said, stepping up behind Allie. "Those were the words he died for."

"He must have been a great man," Allie said.

"He was more than a great man," the lady said. "He was a good man. Honor and faith meant more to him than life. When he died, my life ended."

"He wouldn't want you to feel that way," Allie said. "He would want you to go on living and believing in God."

"I know he would," the lady said. "But I cannot."

"What would it take to make you believe?" Allie asked.

"A miracle," the lady said. The torch sputtered again. She took the second torch from her belt and lit it with the first. "We need to go soon," she said.

"Okay," Allie replied. "Give me just a minute to pray."

"Yes," the lady said. "A minute."

So Allie knelt in the chancel. She prayed that the Kingdom of Gyle could once more become the Kingdom of Gracea. And she prayed for her friend, Lady Galatea. Then she got up from her knees and turned—

"Oh!" Allie said suddenly. "What's that?"

Galatea aimed her torch where Allie pointed. At the edge of the chancel was the ambo, a heavy wooden stand. A large book sat open on the ambo. Allie and Galatea went to look at it.

It was a thick book, bound in leather. Each page was hand-lettered in broad pen strokes, with large, decorated capital letters at the beginning of each chapter. "It must have taken years for someone to letter this book by hand," Allie said.

"The *Biblia Sacra*," Galatea said. "The Holy Bible in the Latin language."

"Look!" Allie said. "This Bible has your name in it!"

Lady Galatea's eyes widened. Allie's finger pointed to a line:

O insensati Galatae! Quis vos fascinavit?

For a brief moment, Galatea thought that Allie was right—that her name was written on a page of the Holy Bible. Then she realized that the word on the page was not Galatea, but Galatae.

"'O foolish Galatians! Who has bewitched you?'" Lady Galatea translated. "Galatae is not my name, Allie. It's the Latin word for Galatians, the people who lived in the region of Galatia."

"But for a moment," Allie said, "you thought the same thing I did. You thought God was talking to you right out of the Bible—and maybe He was. Doesn't it seem like a miracle that this book would be open to this very page?"

"Coincidence is just coincidence," the lady said.

"No, it's *not!*" Allie insisted. "It's a *miracle*. These words *mean* something. 'O foolish Galatea, who has bewitched you?' Who has fooled you into thinking there is no God?"

Galatea turned away. "We've seen enough here," she said. "It's time to go back."

They went back through the crypt and into the maze, following the trail of coins. As they reached each stone, Allie picked up the coin and put it in the bag. The trail of coins made it easy for them to find their way back.

The lady's torch was just beginning to sputter as they climbed the spiral staircase to the top of the tower. Once inside the lady's chamber, they went quickly to bed. Allie was asleep almost as soon as she was snuggled under the blankets of her pallet.

Lady Galatea remained awake and troubled long into the night. A voice seemed to call to her: *O foolish Galatea, who has bewitched you?*

10

FIRE, SMOKE, AND THUNDER

Three days later, King Wyvern entered the cooper's shop with Doctor Delyrius at his side. The shop was cool and shady, and smelled of fresh wood shavings. The cooper sat at his workbench near the front of the shop, smoothing the edge of a barrel stave with a planing tool. He was a heavy-set man with bulging muscles and dark hair and beard. When the cooper looked up and saw King Wyvern, he started to rise.

"Stay, my good man," the king said. "Nothing must hinder your work."

The cooper resumed his work. The king turned to Doctor Delyrius. "What kind of wood is he using? It's not oak."

"A rocket must be light," the Doctor said, "and oak is heavy. I've instructed the cooper to build the rocket barrels out of beechwood. It's light but strong."

The cooper raised the barrel stave to his eye and sighted down the length of it. He grunted his approval, and added it to a stack.

"Let me show you the first completed rocket, Your Majesty," Doctor Delyrius said, guiding the king toward the rear of the shop. "Ah, here it is."

A cigar-shaped wooden rocket rested on wooden sawhorses. It was about ten feet long and made of long, curved strips of beechwood. Just as a wine barrel is held together with metal barrel hoops, the rocket had four metal hoops spaced out along its length. A metal cone at the nose held the explosive warhead. Four stabilizer fins of plate steel projected from the base.

"This doesn't look like the rockets in the book," the king said. "They were not made of wood and iron."

"The rockets in the book," Doctor Delyrius said, "are made of materials we cannot match. But young McCrane has assured me that this wooden rocket will fly—and it will hit the target. He has checked his calculations many times over, and he has been warned of the penalty for failure. I assure you, he has no desire to see his friends suffer."

"Good," the king said, running his hand along the smooth side of the rocket. "I'm happy to see you are training a replacement."

Doctor Delyrius eyed the king darkly. "A replacement?"

"Yes," the king said. "You're an old man, Doctor. Soon it will be time for you to step aside. This young fellow,

McCrane—he's very clever, very gifted. How old is he? Thirteen? Fourteen? Yet he has more knowledge crammed into his young skull than the *learned* Doctor Herendus Delyrius!"

Delyrius scowled. "Though you are the king, *Your Majesty*," he rasped, "you should not mock me." The way he said "Your Majesty" sounded more hateful than any mere insult.

A cruel smile twisted King Wyvern's lips. "Mock you, old friend? After all the years of faithful service you have given me? Why, Doctor, I *praise* you! I compliment you on finding a young apprentice whose reputation will soon over-shadow your own!" The king clapped his hands slowly. "Yes, Doctor, I applaud you."

Eyes smoldering, Doctor Delyrius turned on his heel and stormed out of the cooper's shop.

@ @ @

A cool breeze ruffled Max's brown hair. Standing on a lad-der, Max measured the upright support timber. He marked it by scratching the wood with a piece of iron, then climbed down the ladder. The rocket launching stand had been constructed beside the road in front of the castle. It was nearly finished.

"Do you see where I made the mark?" Max said, turn-ing to the carpenter.

The carpenter was a young man with long, black hair, a lean face, and sinewy arms. "I see the mark," he said.

"The top of the crossbeam must be even with that mark," Max said. "Then anchor the ramp there, at the crossbeam, and down there, at the base of the frame. The angle of the ramp must be *exactly* as I've marked it."

"Aye, it will be," said the carpenter, scratching his head, "though this infernal apparatus makes no sense to me. I've built many siege engines, both catapults and ballistas. But I've never built anything like this. It doesn't *do* anything! There's no fulcrum, no axis, no winch, no sling! What kind of siege engine is this?"

"It's not a siege engine," Max said. "It's just a rocket launching stand. The rocket's going to launch from that ramp, fly through the air, and hit the target a half-mile away." He pointed down the road that led away from the castle gate. A half-mile away, beside the road, was a large mound of rocks, about six feet high.

"Lad," said the carpenter, "I've never known a catapult that could hurl a stone one-fifth that distance." He shook his head. "Hit that mound of stones from here? Hah! Can't be done."

Max shrugged. "We'll see."

The next morning, more than a thousand people gathered on the grassy field in front of the castle gate. Word had spread beyond the castle and throughout the farms and villages: King Wyvern's amazing new weapon was going to be demonstrated in front of Castle Serpenfane.

The wooden rocket sat on its launch ramp, angled toward the sky. A long strip of cloth trailed from its tail. At Max's insistence, a wide area around the rocket stand was roped off in case of an explosion.

Toby and Grady were out on the grass in front of the castle, along with the other knights and squires. Several knights kept people safely away from the rocket. Minstrels and bards passed through the crowd, playing stringed instruments, singing songs, and taking donations for their performances.

A chorus of cheers went up when King Wyvern himself appeared at the parapet over the gatehouse, accompanied by both Doctor Delyrius and the young inventor, Max McCrane.

Allie and Lady Galatea walked out of the lady's chamber and strode alongside the parapet atop the castle wall. "What's happening?" Allie asked. "It looks like some kind of celebration."

"Look there," the lady said, "in front of the drawbridge."

Allie leaned through a gap in the parapet and saw the wooden platform with the king's new weapon sitting on the ramp. Allie laughed. "What is that thing?" she asked. "It looks like a rocket made of wood."

"It is," Galatea said. "I'm told that it was designed by your friend, Max McCrane."

"What?!" Allie's freckled face went pale.

A voice came from the gatehouse above: "Allie!"

Allie looked up and saw Max waving from the top of the gatehouse.

"Allie!" Max said again. "I need to talk to you! After the rocket test!"

"Max!" Allie called back, a wounded look on her face. "Max, what are you doing?"

"Allie, don't be mad," Max said. "I just—" Suddenly, he was yanked away, and Doctor Delyrius appeared.

"Young lady," the Doctor said, "we have a demonstration to perform. Please do not distract my apprentice." Then he was gone.

"You've double-checked your calculations?" Doctor Delyrius asked.

"And triple-checked them," Max replied. "It's a simple matter of thrust, weight, drag, and lift. You just quantify the magnitude of—"

"Yes, yes," the Doctor snapped. "Just as long as it works."

"If you prepared the fuel mixture exactly as I said," Max replied, "it'll work."

From the gatehouse tower, the king gave a signal. The crowd went quiet. A black-clad man on horseback rode across the drawbridge and toward the rocket stand. It was Sir Guy. He held the horse's reins in his left hand and a flaming torch in his right. He halted and looked up to the gatehouse tower.

"Proceed with the launch!" the king ordered.

Sir Guy nodded, then nudged his horse into the roped-off enclosure. The crowd was silent. The air was electric.

Sir Guy swung the torch to the ground, touching the end of the cloth with flame. The cloth caught fire. Sir Guy spurred his horse and swiftly galloped away.

The flame moved along the cloth, up the frame of the rocket stand, and into the rear of the wooden rocket.

KA-FWOOOOM!

Sun-bright flame shot from the tail of the rocket. Clouds of white smoke billowed into the air. The thunder was deafening. The sound wave struck each person as if it were a fist. Hearts forgot to beat. Knees turned to mush.

Trailing a billowy white plume, the rocket streaked skyward. It made a smooth, high arc in the sky—

Then it began to fall.

It hit the target, diving into the mound of stones beside the road. The stone mound vanished in an explosion of smoke and debris.

The sound of the explosion arrived at the castle about two seconds after the blast was seen. It sounded like a massive thunderclap. The echo rang for a long time in the castle walls and faded among the western mountains.

Max pounded his fists against the stone parapet. "Yes! Yes!" he said. "Right on target!" He turned and looked at King Wyvern and Doctor Delyrius.

The king's eyes were wide. The Doctor's face sagged within the hood of his cloak. Both men were stunned.

Max looked down on the grassy field. The wooden rocket stand had caught fire and was burning to the ground. Men, women, and children were running, shouting, screaming, or fainting. Some appeared dazed and disoriented. In moments, the mushrooming cloud of white rocket smoke hid the crowd from Max's sight.

No one had been killed or hurt, but the party atmosphere was over. The people had just seen a demonstration of unimaginable power. They had caught a glimpse of a new kind of war.

And they were afraid.

◎　◎　◎

White smoke billowed over the gatehouse tower, rolling over the parapet, engulfing the Doctor, King Wyvern, and Max. The smoke had a foul, sickening smell—a combination of burning wood and rotten eggs. It stung Max's eyes and throat, and he dashed toward a doorway to escape the fumes. Eyes bleary, he staggered down the stairs, and came out on top of the castle wall. As his eyes cleared, he saw Allie and Lady Galatea ahead of him.

"Allie!" he called, hurrying toward her.

Allie turned and saw him. Her eyes were full of disappointment. While Lady Galatea stayed behind, Allie rushed toward Max.

"Max! Is it true?" she asked. "Are you working for King Wyvern?"

"You don't understand—," Max began, wheezing.

"Then it *is* true!" she said, despairing. "You've joined them! Don't you understand the evil they are doing?"

"Of course I do," Max said, pulling his inhaler from his pocket. "I'm not doing this for them. I'm doing it for you—and for Grady and Toby." He took a puff, then sagged against the parapet.

Allie looked shaken. "What?"

"Doctor Delyrius said I had to help him—or something terrible would happen to all of you."

"Oh, Max!" Allie said. "That's wrong! That's so wrong! Don't you see? I don't want to be saved if it means those rockets are going to be used to kill people. Grady wouldn't want that either."

"Look, Allie," Max said, checking over his shoulder to make sure no one could overhear, "it's not what you think. I don't have it all planned out yet, but I'm trying to figure out a way so that those rockets won't kill anybody." He looked skyward. "I prayed for wisdom, Allie. And I'm doing the best I can."

Suddenly, Allie saw Max as very scared and alone. "I

know, Max," she said. "I'm sorry. I was too hard on you."

"That's okay," Max said. "One more thing: I'm trying to figure out a way to get us all back home. I'm trying to figure out how to fix the Doorway. I know it uses phosphorescent light for power. Toby accidentally turned the Doorway on with one of his glow-in-the-dark eyeballs, and the Doctor used something similar that he calls a moonstone. If I only had one of Toby's eyeballs—"

"There you are!" a gruff voice shouted behind Max. He turned and saw Doctor Delyrius coming out of the gatehouse door, face twisted with rage.

Max turned back to Allie. "I've got to go," he said grimly.

Allie reached out and hugged him. "I'll keep praying for you," she whispered in his ear.

"Max McCrane!" the Doctor roared again.

Max turned and trudged back to Doctor Delyrius.

As Allie watched him go, she heard footsteps behind her and felt Lady Galatea's hands on her shoulders. "Your young friend has the heart of a knight," the lady said. "He reminds me of my Rowland."

11

THE EYE IN THE DOORWAY

Max spent the next few days and nights in the laboratory of Doctor Delyrius. He studied the Doorway, trying to understand how the arrangement of its quartz crystals could turn a wooden doorframe into a time machine. He took his meals in the laboratory. At night, his eyes bleary and his body exhausted, he would curl up on a blanket in front of the furnace. Before he went to sleep, he prayed and he thought—and his thoughts were focused on one problem: how to get himself and his friends back to their own time.

One morning, three days after the rocket test, Max stood in front of the Doorway, vellum and charcoal in hand, sketching a diagram of its light circuit. There were twenty-seven quartz crystals on the front side of the Doorway, twenty-seven quartz crystals on the back, and a brass

receptacle on both sides. He made a note next to the charcoal diagram:

(1) Light enters at receptacle. (2) Light bounces
from crystal to crystal. Must be hollow tunnels in
doorframe for light to travel through. (3) Facets of the
crystals can be turned to reflect light along different
pathways. Maybe a fine-tuning mechanism—turn
crystals different ways to select day and year you
want to go to.

He set the lambskin and charcoal on the lab table and
scratched his head. The more he studied the light pathways
of the Doorway, the more strangely familiar it seemed—

From behind him, Doctor Delyrius interrupted his
thoughts. "Something puzzles me, lad," the Doctor said.

Max turned. "Sir?"

The Doctor leaned close. There was bafflement in his
faded eyes. "How did you and your friends pass through
the Doorway? It requires *light* to work—light from a
moonstone."

"Or from a glow-in-the-dark eyeball," Max said.

The Doctor's bafflement deepened. "A what?"

"A glow-in-the-dark eyeball," Max repeated. "Toby
Brubaker brought a bagful of them to the party." Max
pointed to the brass receptacle in the doorframe. "You put
the moonstone in this thing here, right? Well, Toby put one

of his glow-in-the-dark eyeballs in there—and it worked just like your moonstone. It was an accident—but it made the jewels light up, and it opened a connection between our time and yours."

"Tell me about this glow-in-the-dark eyeball," the Doctor said.

"Well," Max said, "you can get them at any toy store for a buck or two. They're kind of gooshy, and they're coated with phosphorescent paint—glow-in-the-dark paint, probably strontium aluminate. If you put strontium aluminate in the sun for a few hours, it'll glow for twenty, thirty hours straight."

Doctor Delyrius's face sagged. "My moonstone would only glow for a half-hour at most."

"What was it made of?" Max asked.

"I'll show you," the Doctor said. "Close the window and come here."

Max got up and closed the window shutter, then joined Doctor Delyrius at the laboratory table. The room was almost completely dark. The Doctor held a glass retort in his hand. It was round and had a hollow glass tube that bent downward from the top.

"Look," the Doctor said.

At first, Max didn't see anything. Then, as his eyes adjusted to the darkness, he noticed a faint glow in the bottom of the retort.

"That glow comes from tiny traces of the moonstone

substance," Doctor Delyrius said. "I need a hundred times this much to power the Doorway."

"How did you make it?" Max asked.

"I dissolved seashells in aqua fortis, then boiled out the liquid, leaving a dry residue. Then I heated the residue so that it turned yellow. If I leave the yellow residue in bright sunlight, it glows like this."

The glow was feeble, almost impossible to see. Already, it had almost completely faded away.

"You know what that stuff is?" Max said. "Plain old calcium nitrate. You mixed calcium from seashells with nitric acid—what you call *aqua fortis*. It must have taken you forever to make it this way. Where I come from, they make calcium nitrate by the ton."

"The moonstone your friend tossed into the moat," the Doctor said glumly, "took more than six months to make."

"Where did you get the idea for the Doorway?" Max asked. "I mean, how did you figure out how to build it?"

"I made the discovery during my travels thirty years ago," the Doctor said, getting up from the table. He went to a cabinet and rummaged around for something. "I had journeyed to Pergamos in Asia Minor, to study the art of alchemy in the library there. I found a parchment—"

The Doctor pulled out a long sack of stained brown cloth. He opened the sack, pulled out a rolled parchment, and spread it in front of Max. It was brittle and crumbling.

"This is the parchment I found in Pergamos," he said.

"It was written by Theon of Alexandria. Only two copies of this parchment were made. The first disappeared three centuries ago when the Great Library of Alexandria was burned. The second was in the library at Pergamos. I found it—and I took it."

"You *stole* it!" Max said. "Just like you stole that book from my dad's study!"

"Knowledge doesn't belong on dusty shelves, lad," the Doctor said with rising annoyance. "Knowledge belongs in the hands of those who will use it to shape the world."

It seemed to Max that thieves always have an excuse for their thievery. He looked closely at the parchment, which was filled with writing and drawings in a faint brown ink.

"The parchment is in Theon's own hand," the Doctor said. "It contains plans for building his time-journeying device in various shapes—a chariot, a boat, and of course, a Doorway."

"I don't understand the writing," Max said. "Is it Greek?"

"Yes," the Doctor snapped impatiently.

"This is the complete plan for the Doorway!" Max said. "It tells you how to cut the quartz crystals, how to build the Doorway, how to make the moonstone—everything! It's all right here! You didn't think up anything yourself! You *stole* the whole idea from this Theon guy!"

Doctor Delyrius angrily snatched up the parchment and stuffed it back in the sack. "Yes, yes, yes! I stole the idea! And I built the Doorway!"

"But you don't know how it works, do you?" Max said. "You don't understand the scientific principles involved. You just copied this guy's work. Don't you understand what the Doorway is, Doctor?"

The Doctor looked helplessly at Max—then shook his head.

"The Doorway," Max replied, "is a *Timebender*."

"A Timebender?" the Doctor said.

Max pointed to the Doorway. "This Theon guy used a series of crystals to channel light in a certain pattern around a doorway—a four-dimensional pattern called a Klein bottle. I did the same thing with flashlight batteries, light-emitting diodes, optical fibers, and a Volkswagen Beetle."

The old man seemed hopelessly confused. "What kind of beetle?"

"Never mind," Max said with a sigh. "The only thing that matters is that the Doorway won't work without phosphorescent light."

"I've tried candlelight," the Doctor said, "but—"

"I know," Max said. "Candlelight flickers. Timebending requires a steady, constant light source." He pointed to the golden Doorway with its darkened crystals. "Without a moonstone or a glow-in-the-dark eyeball, that thing is just a Doorway to nowhere."

Max awoke to the sound of hushed voices. It was dark in the laboratory. From the sound of their voices, he could tell that two men were in the room: Doctor Delyrius and King Wyvern.

"What if the boy hears us, Doctor?"

"He sleeps soundly. Speak softly, and he won't awaken."

Max closed his eyes—but kept his ears perked up.

"So," the king said, "we only have enough fuel for three rockets."

"True," the Doctor said. "The first ingredient of rocket fuel is nitrum flammans—and I've already used every ounce I had. I can buy more from Jabir the Peddler in four weeks. Meanwhile, three rockets will be more than enough to defeat the Kingdom of Elysia. Let me show you on the maps."

Max heard a rustling of parchment.

"Position the rockets here, here, and here," the Doctor said. "Hide the rocket launching stands behind these woods. Aim the first rocket at the portcullis, and you will bring down the gatehouse. Use the second and third rockets against the corner towers, and you'll probably collapse the entire front wall."

"Very well, Doctor," King Wyvern said, "you have convinced me. I shall go and give the order to the captain of my knights. We shall assemble the army and march on Elysia."

Max kept his eyes shut as the king walked past and left the laboratory. Max decided that, the first chance he got, he was going to take a look at those maps.

The next morning, there was a knock at the door of Lady Galatea's chamber. The lady opened the door. A short, plump woman in a pale blue dress stood at the threshold. Her face was framed by a wimple of white cloth. She had an empty basket in her hands. "Good day, milady," the woman said. "Good day, Miss Allie. I'm here for the laundry."

"Oh, thank you, thank you!" Allie said, grabbing up a pile of clothes by the foot of the bed. "My overalls were getting pretty grungy before Lady Galatea found some other clothes for me to wear."

She dashed to the door with the laundry in her arms. As she placed the bundle in the laundrywoman's basket, something fell out of the pocket of her overalls. The thing was round, and it hit the floor with a *squish*.

Allie bent and picked it up. "Well, how do you like that?" she said, holding the object out.

The lady and the laundrywoman *screamed!* The thing in Allie's hand was *staring* at them!

It was an eyeball.

"Oops, sorry!" Allie said. "It's just a toy—see?"

The two women bent and examined the thing in Allie's hand. "It looks—evil," Lady Galatea said.

"Well, it is kind of nasty, all right," Allie said. "I wonder how it got in my—oh, now I remember! I found a bunch of these eyeballs on the pizza, and I stuck one of them in my pocket without thinking!" She shaded the eyeball with her left hand. "It's been in my overalls for days! It's not glowing anymore! Excuse me, I've got to put this in the sunshine!" She rushed past the two women and was gone.

"What an odd girl!" the laundrywoman said.

"She certainly is," Lady Galatea said. "She's always talking, and nothing she says makes any sense!"

◎ ◎ ◎

Doctor Delyrius was out of the laboratory.

Whenever the Doctor was gone, Max took out a piece of lambskin vellum and copied notes from the Doctor's hand-written journals and parchments. Max already had collected a long list of the Doctor's astronomical observations—comets, eclipses, and the motions of planets. If he ever got back to his own time, that information would come in handy. . . .

Max heard footsteps on the staircase. Someone was coming up to the laboratory! Max closed the Doctor's journal and stuffed the parchment in his pocket.

The door opened—

But the person who entered was not Doctor Delyrius. It was—

"Lady Galatea!" Max said.

"Max McCrane," the lady said, "I've brought something

for you—a gift from Allie." She reached into the folds of her cloak, pulled something out, and offered it to Max in her open hand.

An eyeball. A *glowing* eyeball.

Max stared in astonishment. "I don't believe it!" he said, taking the eyeball from the lady's outstretched hand. "Where did Allie find it?"

"It was in the pocket of her all-overs," the lady said.

"Her what?" Max asked—then it dawned on him what she meant. "Oh! You mean her *overalls!*"

"Her overalls, yes," said the lady. "Allie said you would be—how did she put it? She said you would be 'sooo freaked out' to receive it."

"I am!" Max said, squeezing the eyeball excitedly. "This is so cool! Thanks! I mean, really! Thanks!"

The lady smiled faintly. "I suppose it's a good-luck charm of some sort."

"Better!" Max said. "It's an answer to prayer!"

"Well, good-bye, Max," the lady said, turning to leave.

"Good-bye, ma'am," Max said, grinning broadly while bouncing the eyeball in his hand. "And thanks again!" He shoved the eyeball in his pocket.

The lady left, closing the door behind her.

The moment the door snicked shut, Max went to the Doctor's cabinet and took out the rolled maps. He found one that showed the Kingdom of Gyle, the Kingdom of

Elysia, and various castles, towns, rivers, and natural land-marks. He rolled the map tightly and stuffed it in his shirt.

He bit his lip, regretting the fact that he would have to leave his friends in the Middle Ages—

But what else could he do?

He went to the golden Doorway, sent up a silent prayer, then took the eyeball from his pocket and placed it in the brass receptacle.

The Doorway lit up. Pale yellow-green light poured from its quartz crystals. It was time to go. Max opened the heavy wooden door. The veil of darkness yawned before him like a black hole.

The darkness between the centuries.

Then Max heard footsteps again—not the light, quick footsteps of Lady Galatea this time, but the heavy trudge of Doctor Delyrius. There was no time to lose.

Ahead of Max, through the open Doorway, was a cur-tain of darkness. Max put one foot through the Doorway. Beyond the darkness, his foot rested on something soft and springy—

Yes! It was the Persian rug in the study! One of Max's feet was already home! He had one foot in the past, and one foot in the future.

Behind Max, the laboratory door opened and Doctor Delyrius walked in. The old man's jaw dropped. He saw Max half-swallowed by the darkness of the open Doorway.

He saw the Doorway's crystals all brightly lit. "No!" the old man shrieked. "No!" And he ran toward Max.

Max was about to leap through the Doorway—then he remembered the eyeball. *I can't let the Doctor have the eyeball!* He reached for the eyeball, trying to snatch it from the brass receptacle as he fell through the Doorway and into the darkness—

But as Max fell back into his own world, the clawlike fingers of Doctor Delyrius raked his arm, pushing his hand away from the eyeball. Max landed heavily on the Persian rug of his father's study. He jumped to his feet and turned. He was back in his own time!

Then he saw Doctor Delyrius materialize in the open Doorway. The Doctor's eyes were wild and stormy, filled with rage, hate, and—strangely—a gleam of triumph.

"I'm rid of you," the Doctor roared, "forever!" The Doctor grabbed the door handle and retreated back to his own time, pulling the door shut with a resounding slam.

The Doorway still glowed with yellow-green light.

Then Max remembered: There was an eyeball in the receptacle on this side of the door. Max, Allie, and Grady had left it there when they were pulled through the Doorway. Max ran to the Doorway and snatched the eyeball out of the metal receptacle, and the crystals went dark.

Just to make sure, Max opened the Doorway—

And stared into a closet full of cardboard boxes.

The connection to the past was broken.

12

THE ROCKET WAR

The armored caravan left Castle Serpenfane a few days later. First came the advance guard, led by King Wyvern himself. He was followed by the knights on horseback, with their captain, Sir Osbert; the knights' shield-bearers, the squires, on foot; the surveyors and scouts, also on foot. Toby and Grady walked among the squires, carrying shields on their backs. Lady Galatea and Allie also rode with the advance guard.

Next came the rear guard. These were the foot soldiers—castle watchmen, tradesmen, servants, yeomen, and serfs. Some came from the villages and countryside around the Kingdom of Gyle. The supply carts, weapons carts, and pack animals followed at the very end.

From his tower window, Doctor Delyrius watched the departure of the caravan of war. He was an old man and he no longer liked to travel. He would wait in Castle Serpenfane to receive news of King Wyvern's glorious victory.

The first day's march lasted from sunup until mid-afternoon—about nine hours of walking with three stops for bread, water, and rest. The armored caravan covered over twenty miles, then camped on the banks of the River Cyderwyn. The second morning, after fording the Cyderwyn, the company marched nine more hours. Their road skirted the east side of Esmour Knoll, then bent west of Wearyall Hill. The company made camp beside the river Went. The third day began with the crossing of the Wentford Bridge. King Wyvern was the first to cross the bridge, and he did so with his sword in his hand—an official act of war.

So the forces of the Kingdom of Gyle crossed into the Kingdom of Elysia and advanced toward Engelwick Castle.

"They're supposed to launch the rockets just before dawn," Grady said, sitting by a campfire in the meadow. "Then the battle begins."

"I say there won't be any battle," said Piers. "You saw what one rocket can do. Whoosh! Boom! Whatever it hits disappears!"

"Right," said the littlest squire, Henry the Lesser, sitting on a log. "Though I hope they put up *some* kind of fight! I haven't seen real blood in ever so long!"

Piers gave Henry a shove, knocking him off the log. "Who are you fooling, runt? You'd fall in a swoon at the sight of blood!"

"I would not!" shouted Henry, jumping to his feet. "I've seen plenty of blood! Buckets of it! I'm not scared of anything—not even you, Piers!"

Grady jumped up and leaped between Piers and Henry the Lesser. "Knock it off, guys!" he warned. "We're not here to fight each other."

"Nobody calls me a coward!" Henry the Lesser shouted. "Nobody!"

"Look, everybody's scared," Grady said. "I'm sure scared—I've never seen a lot of blood or guys hacking at each other with swords. So, I'm plenty scared."

"Stubblefield—," Toby said.

"But there's nothing wrong with being scared," Grady said. "It's how you handle your fear that decides whether you're a coward or a hero. You guys just have to get your minds off of swords and blood and—"

"Stubblefield!" Toby said more insistently.

"What is it, Toby?"

"Don't talk about swords and blood and stuff, okay?" Toby said.

"Why not?"

"Because one time," Toby said, "I had to have a blood test, and the doctor poked my finger, and when I saw that drop of blood on my finger—"

Toby tottered, then fell sideways onto the grass.

Grady bent down at Toby's side. "Hey, he fainted!"

Most of the knights rode black Friesian war-horses, with high, arched necks and long, wavy tails. Allie and Lady Galatea, however, rode dappled palfrey horses. At the end of the day's march, Allie and the lady walked their horses in the meadow to cool them off, then tied them to a pair of birch trees at the edge of the meadow. As their horses rested in the shade, Allie and Galatea took brushes from their saddlebags and groomed the animals.

"Milady," Allie said, "isn't there any way to stop this war?"

"That is a matter for the king to decide," the lady said, "and he has made his decision."

"But he is an *evil* king!" Allie said.

Lady Galatea paled and looked around, afraid someone might have overheard. "You must never say such a thing aloud!" she hissed.

"But King Wyvern serves a false god," Allie persisted. "The Silver Dragon!"

The lady grasped Allie's arm. "And just what would you have me do? Can one woman stop a war? Can one woman change the will of a king?"

"Maybe not," Allie said, "but one person can take a stand for what's right."

Lady Galatea searched Allie's eyes. "King Wyvern is my sovereign liege, and my duty is to serve him, no matter what he commands."

"But if the king is wrong—"

"You speak nonsense," the lady said. "A king cannot be wrong! If the king speaks it, it is the law!"

"When a king steals the faith of his people," Allie said, "and forbids them to worship the one true God, then he's an *evil* king—and he must be opposed!"

"The one true God, Allie?" the lady retorted. "Who is to say what is true? There have been many gods in this land. The Druids practiced human sacrifice and prayed to the earth, fire, water, and trees. Then came the Norsemen and their strange, bloody gods—Odin, Thor, Tyr, and the rest. Then the Romans came to this land, bringing Jupiter and Juno, Mars and Venus, Apollo and Diana—gods so corrupt that the Romans themselves had no respect for them."

"But the Christians—," Allie said.

"Ah, yes!" the lady said. "Then came the Christians, and the story they told was beautiful, and at one time I hoped it might be true—the story of a God of love, and a Son who died, and a tomb that was empty. Such a beautiful story, Allie—but then, aren't all fairy tales beautiful?"

"That story is not a fairy tale," Allie said. "It's a miracle!"

"A miracle!" Lady Galatea laughed with derision. "Am I supposed to believe in miracles? I have never seen one. In this world, I have seen only sorrow and death. My

Rowland was pierced with a sword, and he went into the tomb, and he never came out. Where is my miracle, Allie? Where is the miracle that will make a believer out of me?"

"Milady," Allie said, "if only you would—"

"Allie," the woman interrupted, "only a miracle can convince me that your King, your God, exists. Unless I see your God perform a miracle, I have no king but King Wyvern."

The forces of Gyle arose long before the sun came up and assembled on the road by torchlight. Squires helped their knights prepare for battle. The knights put on chain mail hauberks that covered them from throat to knees. Iron helmets covered their heads. They strapped on swords and battle-axes, then mounted their horses. The squires handed up their lances and shields.

Once the knights were mounted, torches were extinguished and the column advanced toward Engelwick Castle by starlight alone. King Wyvern rode at the head of the column, mounted on a magnificent dapple-gray Percheron stallion. As they advanced, King Wyvern turned to Sir Osbert. "On this day," he said, "we will change the nature of warfare forever."

"Yes, my liege," Sir Osbert said.

"When I conquered the Kingdom of Esperaunce," King

Wyvern said, "the siege lasted forty days and cost me a small fortune—not to mention the lives of many soldiers. You can't imagine what it costs to train replacement soldiers these days—a frightful expense! And then there was the siege of Castle Warburton. It lasted five weeks—and the plunder scarcely yielded a wagonload of gold and silver. Hardly worth the bother! But this day will be glorious, Sir Osbert! We simply launch a few rockets, slaughter half the enemy's forces with a single strike, then ride home with our wagons bulging with gold!"

"Yes, my liege," Sir Osbert said.

The road took the column of knights and soldiers through the dark woods and out to the edge of a broad, grassy plain—and there it was: Engelwick Castle. A river ran through the middle of the valley, and the castle rose up on the far bank. Engelwick was a rock-ribbed fortress of strength. Her walls, towers, and spires glowed dimly under a moonless sky. The drawbridge was down, spanning the river. And why not? The Kingdom of Elysia was at peace with all its neighbors.

The king led the column out into the valley.

Allie and Lady Galatea rode their horses just behind the knights. Allie thought she had never seen anything so beautiful in her life—the soft brilliance of the Milky Way overhead; the valley below, a dim landscape painted in shadows and blue starlight. It broke Allie's heart to know that this peaceful beauty would soon be horribly shattered.

Not far behind, Toby and Grady marched with the squires. The squires were expected to move to the edge of the battlefield when the fighting began and to give aid to any knights who were wounded. Most of the squires had seen battles before, but Toby and Grady didn't know what to expect. All they knew was that if King Wyvern got his way, they would soon see a battlefield choked with blood, death, and horror.

The column clanked and clopped and tramped along the road until the castle was only a hundred yards away— about as far away as the length of a football field. At the head of the column, King Wyvern nodded to his standard-bearer. The standard-bearer raised his bugle, and a high, clear note echoed across the valley.

The signal for war had been given. Nothing could stop it now.

Moments later, the first rocket exploded out of the forest behind the soldiers and to their right. It burst into the sky on a column of white-hot fire. The entire valley was lit up by the glare, and Engelwick Castle shone like silver.

All along the column of knights and foot soldiers, shouts and cheers of triumph went up, only to be drowned out by the thunder of the rocket. King Wyvern raised his sword to the sky and shouted, "Fire and thunder, smite Engelwick to smoke and rubble! Destroy my enemy in the name of the Dragon!"

Watching the rocket climb, Allie felt a shadow of despair

come over her. She had hoped Max had found a way to sab-
otage the rockets before he disappeared. But when the first
rocket roared into the sky, Allie's hopes died.

Then came a blast from the forest on the left, and the
landscape lit up once more, nearly as bright as day. The
second wooden rocket was blazing into the sky. Another
blast to the left, and the third wooden rocket was rising, its
fiery tail blindingly bright, its thunder deafeningly loud.

The first rocket reached the top of its arc, then began to fall
toward the castle gatehouse. The second rocket also began to
fall, aimed at the castle tower on the left. Then the third rocket
began its descent toward the castle tower on the right.

The first rocket blossomed in a brilliant explosion that
lit up the night sky. Its glare was so bright, it hurt the eyes,
like a glance at the sun. The sound of the blast shook every
soldier of Gyle to the pit of his stomach.

The second rocket exploded.

The third rocket exploded.

The thunder of the explosions seemed to roll and echo
forever. At King Wyvern's command, the column quick-
ened its pace.

Before them, Engelwick Castle stood wreathed in smoke—
But undamaged.

Undamaged?!

The column stopped in the road, though no order was
given to halt. King Wyvern stared up at the castle towers, not
believing his eyes. He had seen the flash of the explosions

and had heard their thunder. The walls in front of him should have been piles of rubble—but they were completely untouched.

Then, from the castle, came a grinding, groaning sound. It was the sound of the raising of the massive iron gate, the portcullis. As the King of Gyle and his knights watched in amazement, clouds of eerie gray fog rolled out of the opening. The fog rolled across the river and the draw-bridge, and out toward the army of King Wyvern.

"What kind of enchantment—!" the king whispered.

Brilliant beams of colored light—shining lances of blue, red, green, and yellow—pierced the fog and shone in the eyes of the king and his knights. From atop the castle walls and gatehouse, powerful lights cast a dazzling white glare on the army of Gyle. Then, out of the fog that billowed from the castle gate, ghostly shadows appeared—shadows of armored knights on horseback.

"Ghosts!" the horror-stricken king whispered. "Shadows of slain knights! This kingdom is haunted!"

"What shall we do, my liege?" Sir Osbert groaned. "We cannot make war against an army of ghosts!"

A thunderous noise exploded from the castle, like the wailing of tortured spirits. It was a screeching, screaming, shrieking sound, unlike anything ever heard before upon the earth. It was a sound that made hundreds of human hearts melt like wax. It was the sound of—

@ @ @

"Creed!" Allie said in amazement. She turned to Lady Galatea and saw that the woman's eyes were wide with terror. "Don't be afraid, milady!" she shouted as the noise rolled over them. "It's music, milady, music!"

"What?" the lady shouted back, pale and bewildered.

"It's a song!" Allie screamed with joy. "It's 'Freedom Fighter' by Creed! Max came through! Woohoo!"

Drums pounded. Electric guitars wailed. "Can't you hear us coming? / The fight has only just begun!" declared the raging voice of a singer who would not be born for a thousand years to come.

Allie looked up at the sky and saw clouds of gray smoke hanging over the castle—and she knew that Max had somehow found a way to make the rockets explode harm-lessly in midair. "You did it, Max! I don't know how, but you did it!"

Fog continued rolling across the meadow as the smoke from the rockets settled toward the ground. Everywhere, the landscape was becoming hazy and indistinct. "Milady!" she called. "If we stay here, we'll get caught in all that smoke! Come with me!" She spurred her pal-frey forward, and a bewildered Lady Galatea followed.

@ @ @

King Wyvern knew the battle was lost, but he was so terrified that he didn't even think to order a retreat. The road behind him was clogged with confused and frightened foot soldiers. Ahead of him, riders approached out of the mist.

"KING WYVERN!"

Those words came in a voice so loud that it echoed from the mountains. King Wyvern's horse reared up, its forehooves pawing the air. He lost his grip on the reins and fell to the ground. His sword slipped from his fingers and tumbled into the darkness.

"KING WYVERN! SURRENDER IMMEDIATELY—OR FORFEIT YOUR LIFE!"

The king clambered to his feet and tried to remount his horse, but the frightened Percheron took off at a gallop. The knights saw their king swordless and unhorsed, and heard a supernaturally loud voice demanding his surrender—so they, too, galloped away into the forest. The king was abandoned as the tendrils of fog closed around him.

"KING WYVERN! SURRENDER NOW!"

Terrorized, his knees turned to mush, his heart a throbbing lump in his throat, King Wyvern staggered among shifting shadows, groping through fog and smoke. He cast a quick glance over his shoulder and saw the ghostly knights riding out upon the meadow. The king turned, panic-stricken, and plunged into the dark forest.

"SURRENDER!"

King Wyvern stumbled in the dark and fell headlong

onto the ground. His helmet fell off and rolled away in the darkness. He climbed to his feet, a moan of fear escaping his trembling lips—and he fell again. He turned, peering through the gray fog—

And saw a ghostly shape approaching on foot, cloaked and hooded, sword raised. The pursuer was only a few yards away.

The king got up once more on his unsteady feet—

And ran into a tree trunk. "Unnngh!" He stopped and turned, swaying. His forehead ached, his vision was double, and his ears were ringing.

The shape that pursued the king now had him cornered, backed against a tree. In the shifting lights that pierced the fog and smoke, King Wyvern caught a brief glimpse of the face of his pursuer. His eyes flickered with recognition. "You!"

"Wyvern," Lady Galatea said, "I claim you as my prisoner." She held the point of her sword against his chest, and he backed up against the tree.

"This is treason!" the king croaked.

"This is justice!" the lady replied.

"But I am your king!"

"My King," she answered, "is the Lord of Creation."

"But why?" the king asked. "Why have you turned against me?"

"Because," the lady answered, "I have witnessed a miracle."

The king's mouth opened and closed—but no sound came out. He was not only utterly defeated—he was utterly baffled.

"Allie!" Lady Galatea called.

"Coming, milady!" Allie answered, running among the trees. She arrived carrying a length of heavy cord. "I found the cord in your saddlebag."

The lady motioned to the king. "Turn around!" she snapped.

"You'll forfeit your life for this!" the king snarled, turning his face to the tree.

Allie handed the cord to the lady. "Woohoo!" she whooped. "Girl power!"

Lady Galatea passed her sword to Allie. "If he moves," the lady said, "run this through his gizzard." The lady knew Allie could never run a sword through anyone's "gizzard"—but the king didn't know that.

Allie held the sword while the lady tied the king's hands behind his back. Then Allie and the lady led their prisoner back toward the castle.

As they emerged into the clearing, Allie saw the eastern sky growing brighter. The sun would be up before long, and the fog and smoke would clear.

It was going to be a beautiful day.

"Come on, Toby," Grady said. "Let's go to the castle! I haven't figured it all out yet, but I know something good has happened."

"What about those guys?" Toby asked. He pointed to a pair of ghostly knights riding toward them out of the fog. "They've got their swords out! Dude, they're going to kill us!"

"In the name of Queen Marielle of Elysia," called one of the knights, "I bid you peace!"

"Look, Toby!" Grady said. "They're not ghosts. It's just the fog that made them look so spooky."

The knights were dressed in white, with helmets and swords of polished steel. One rode a white horse, the other a dappled gray. The symbol of the cross was emblazoned in red upon their pure white shields.

The knight who had greeted them spoke again. "You must be Grady—and you are Toby. We came to take you to Engelwick Castle."

Toby's jaw dropped. "Dude! How did you know our names?"

The other knight said, "Max McCrane told us how to recognize you."

"Max!" Grady shouted. "That explains everything!"

The knights lifted the boys onto their horses and rode back through the fog, toward Engelwick Castle.

King Wyvern trudged across the grassy clearing. If he walked too slowly, he felt Lady Galatea's sword point nip at his back. The lady and Allie led their horses by the reins as they marched their captive to Engelwick Castle. Reaching the drawbridge, they were joined by several white-clad knights of the Kingdom of Elysia. Prodding the defeated king forward, they crossed the drawbridge and came to the front gate of the castle.

"Max!" Allie shouted. She handed the reins of her palfrey to the lady, then ran to Max. He was standing in the castle courtyard, hands in his pockets, a big grin across his face. Behind him was Timebender, his battered orange Volkswagen Beetle. Next to him stood a lady—tall, fair-skinned, fair-haired, and radiant. She was dressed in a long white robe and red cloak and had a thin gold circlet in her hair.

Allie ran to Max and threw her arms around him. "Oh, Max, I didn't know if I was ever going to see you again!"

Max reddened. "Uh, Allie," he said, "I'd like you to meet Queen Marielle of the Kingdom of Elysia. Your Majesty, this is my friend, Allie."

"Oh!" Allie said, putting her hand to her mouth. "Oh, my! I—I don't even know how to curtsy!"

Queen Marielle smiled graciously. "That is not necessary," she said. "I'm pleased to meet you, Allie. Your friend Max has told me a great deal about you these past three days."

Allie's eyes widened. "Three days! Max, you've been here for three days!"

"Yeah," Max said. "It took time to get everything set up—the strobe lights, lasers, fog machines, and music."

Just then, Lady Galatea approached with King Wyvern. "Your Majesty," the lady said, "here is the man who attacked your kingdom."

"King Wyvern," Queen Marielle said coldly, "in my treasury room is a parchment with your signature and seal upon it—a treaty of peace between our two kingdoms. It is deeply disappointing to learn how little you value your word and sacred honor."

The king looked at Max strangely. "You!" he said in disbelief. "You did this to me?"

Max shrugged. "How does it feel," he asked, "to get beaten by a middle-schooler?" Then Max took something out of his pocket and put it to his lips: a wireless microphone. He spoke—

And his voice boomed like thunder: "KING WYVERN! SURRENDER! KING WYVERN, YOU ARE A ROYAL DOOFUS! KING WYVERN—!" And Max could contain himself no longer. He doubled up in uncontrollable laughter.

The king stared dumbly at Max, and his eyes got wider and wider—

Queen Marielle motioned to a pair of her knights. "Take this man into your custody," she said. The knights came, grasped King Wyvern by both arms, and led him away.

Allie stepped forward with Lady Galatea at her side. "Your Majesty," Allie said, "I would like to present my friend Lady Galatea."

The lady knelt before the queen and presented her

sword, hilt first. "I surrender myself to your mercy," she said, "and present my sword."

"I do not want your sword," the queen said, "only your friendship. Arise, Lady Galatea. We have much to talk about."

The queen and the lady began walking across the courtyard, toward the splendid palace of Elysia. As the queen talked, the lady got a very surprised look on her face . . .

"Grady!" Max shouted. "And Toby!"

Two white-clad knights rode through the gate with Toby and Grady seated behind them. The knights helped Toby and Grady to the ground. Max ran over and clapped them both on the back.

"How did you do it, Max?" Grady asked. "How did you get the rockets to explode in midair?"

"Oh, that was easy," Max said. "It was just a simple matter of fuel, thrust, and altitude control. I designed the rockets to launch at a *forty-five*-degree angle, burn fuel for five-point-three seconds, and explode at the target. That's why the first test hit the target so perfectly. But then I told the carpenter to build the launching stands at a *fifty-five*-degree angle—ten degrees too high. The rockets launched at too steep an angle, and when the warheads exploded, the rockets were high and short of the target.

Instead of a big castle-busting bomb, you've got a big fireworks display."

"Well, that explains that," Allie said. "And the strobe lights, lasers, and fog machines are from the party, right?"

"Right," Max said. "The Doorway took me back home—" He thumbed over his shoulder at the Volkswagen. "And Timebender brought me back. I took the astronomical observations and maps of Doctor Delyrius, fed the information into my computer, and I was able to pinpoint the exact time and place I needed to return to."

"Dude!" Toby said. "That means I can go home! Come on, McCrane, take me back home so I can get some burgers and fries!"

"We can't go home yet," Max said. "I have some unfinished business—with Doctor Delyrius."

13

THE STRANGE DISAPPEARANCE
OF DOCTOR DELYRIUS

Allie and Lady Galatea walked along the riverbank, stepping over moss-green stones and admiring the pale-pink flowers of the whortleberry bushes that grew there. To Allie, the entire world seemed like an enchanted fairyland, drenched in sparkling liquid sunlight.

"I'm sorry I can't tell you what Queen Marielle and I talked about," the lady said, "but you'll know very soon. The queen said it would only be a secret for a little while."

"That's okay," Allie said. "What I really want to know is—what changed you? I mean, all of a sudden, you believed in God and you turned against King Wyvern. Why?"

"Oh, Allie!" Lady Galatea said. "You really don't know?"

Allie shook her head.

"I saw a miracle!" the lady said.

"What miracle?" Allie asked. "The rockets exploding in

midair? The lights and fog? Or Max time-traveling to meet us here in his Volkswagen? Because those aren't miracles, you know. Everything that happened has a perfectly logical, scientific explanation."

"Allie," Galatea said, "let me ask you something: What is a miracle?"

"Well . . ." Allie paused. "I'd say a miracle is a wonderful event that is totally unexpected, maybe even impossible—but it happens because God arranges for it to happen according to His Eternal Plan."

The lady smiled. "What a beautiful way to express it! Yes, that's it exactly! And didn't we see miracles today? Wonderful events, totally unexpected, but part of God's plan? Did you expect those rockets to explode in midair? Did you expect to see a strange fog and weird lights and loud music? Everything that happened this morning was the most unexpected thing that could have happened. And the fact that God used your friend Max to make it happen doesn't make it any less of a miracle."

"I guess you're right, milady," Allie said.

"And God has used you to change my heart," the lady said, "and that's a miracle, too! Ever since you came here, you've been trying to show me the truth, and I've been closing my eyes to it. When we were in the chapel, and you showed me those words—'O insensati Galatae! Quis vos fascinavit?'—I almost believed that God Himself was speaking to me, to Galatea, right from the pages of that book. And that's because He *was!* And that was a miracle, too! So many miracles—but I refused to see them. The only miracle that could penetrate this hardened heart of mine was a miracle of bright lights, loud noises, and explosions in the sky."

"What about Sir Rowland?" Allie asked. "What about your grief?"

"That's the most wonderful miracle of all," Galatea said. "Now that I believe, I know I'll see my beloved Rowland again."

She stopped and turned, taking Allie's face in her hands. Allie looked into Galatea's eyes—eyes that were once so hard and distant, eyes that refused to cry. Those eyes were wet now, and the long-denied tears finally came spilling down Galatea's face.

Miraculously, they were tears of joy.

The knights of Queen Marielle rounded up many of those who had come to make war. They were allowed to make camp on the broad green meadow in front of Engelwick Castle. Then the Queen of Elysia came out to the meadow with Lady Galatea at her side, as well as a number of knights and nobles of her court.

"Let it be made known to you," the queen said, "that the King of Gyle has been dethroned, and shall be tried for the crimes against the Kingdom of Elysia. Also let it be known to you that the Kingdom of Gyle has been dissolved and is no more."

A murmur went through the crowd.

"Henceforth," the queen continued, "you shall be citizens of the Kingdom of Gracea. That is the name by which the Kingdom of Gyle was formerly known, and by which it shall be known again. And for her part in capturing the rogue King of Gyle, Lady Galatea shall henceforth be known as Queen Galatea, Empress of Gracea. May she rule with wisdom and grace, and may there always be peace and friendship between the people of Elysia and the people of Gracea."

There was a long moment of astonished silence—and then a cheer went up from the citizens of the restored Kingdom of Gracea. The cheer was loud and long.

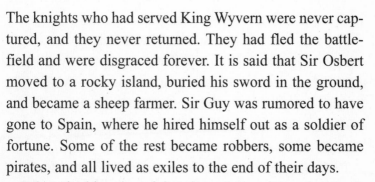

The knights who had served King Wyvern were never captured, and they never returned. They had fled the battlefield and were disgraced forever. It is said that Sir Osbert moved to a rocky island, buried his sword in the ground, and became a sheep farmer. Sir Guy was rumored to have gone to Spain, where he hired himself out as a soldier of fortune. Some of the rest became robbers, some became pirates, and all lived as exiles to the end of their days.

When the histories of that time were written, the attack

upon the Kingdom of Elysia was sometimes called "The War That Never Was." It was a war in which no one died, and only one man was taken prisoner.

The day after The War That Never Was, the people of Gracea departed for home. Queen Galatea and her friend Allie O'Dell rode their palfreys side by side at the front of the procession.

"What's the first thing you'll do as queen?" Allie asked.

The new queen didn't even have to think about her answer. "I'm going to do five things at once," Queen Galatea said. "I will order all the images of the Silver Dragon removed from the castle and destroyed. I will order the chapel reopened and dedicate my life and my reign to the service of the one true King. I will restore the castle's original name—Castle Mageste, in honor of the majesty of our Creator. I will liberate all the kingdoms and people who were conquered by King Wyvern. And I will return all the gold, silver, jewels, and other goods that were looted and stolen by King Wyvern."

Next in the procession came Timebender, Max's ugly orange Volkswagen. It was pulled along by a pair of black Friesian stallions as if it were a grand carriage. Max sat in the driver's seat, with Grady next to him. Toby sat in the backseat. The fog machines, stereo speakers, lasers, and strobe lights were stowed under the hood.

Following Timebender was a column of hundreds of people. They talked, laughed, and sang as they walked.

The people were happy to be going home to their villages and farms, happy to finally be citizens of a land at peace.

When the procession arrived at the gates of Castle Serpenfane, the watchmen of the gatehouse shouted, "What news of the war against Elysia?"

"Wyvern is defeated," Queen Galatea answered, "and is a prisoner of Queen Marielle. His knights are scattered like chaff upon the wind. I am now your queen, and this land is the Kingdom of Gracea once more."

"What?" said a grating voice from a high tower window—the voice of Doctor Delyrius. "What's that you say? King Wyvern defeated? Impossible!"

Max leaned out the window of Timebender. "Doctor Delyrius!" he shouted. "I want to talk to you!"

"It can't be!" Doctor Delyrius shrieked from the tower window. "McCrane! Why do you torment me?"

"Doctor, I only want to—"

"No! No! No!" the Doctor wailed. He slammed the shutter of the window and was gone.

Queen Galatea called to the gatehouse. "Watchman! As your queen, I bid you—raise the portcullis!"

There was a pause—then the watchman called down, "Yes, Your Majesty."

The queen and Allie were the first to enter, followed by Max, Grady, and Toby in the horse-drawn Volkswagen. As the car came to a halt in the middle of the courtyard, Max jumped out and ran to the door of the tower that housed the

Doctor's laboratory. He was out of breath and wheezing as he reached the top of the staircase. He paused to take a quick puff from his inhaler. Then he opened the door of the laboratory and walked in.

"Doctor Delyrius?" he called.

The laboratory was dark. There was no one there.

At the far end of the laboratory, the golden Doorway stood, its crystals glowing. Max walked over to the Doorway and took the glow-in-the-dark eyeball out of the brass receptacle. The Doorway went dark.

Max looked closely at the quartz crystals and saw that the Doctor had changed their alignment. Max had memorized the correct alignment for his own time, and this was clearly different. He wondered for a moment what era Doctor Delyrius had dialed into those crystals, then he shrugged. Wherever the Doorway had sent the strange old alchemist, at least it wasn't Max's own time.

Max turned and walked out of the laboratory, closing the door behind him.

The four time travelers stood in front of Timebender, ready to return to the twenty-first century. They had taken time to bathe and scrub, and Queen Galatea's friend, the laundrywoman, had washed their clothes for them. Each of them looked as clean and fresh as they had when they disappeared from the party at Max's house.

Queen Galatea was on hand to see them off. So were Piers, Henry the Lesser, and the other squires.

Allie turned to Queen Galatea. "I wish we could phone each other. Or even e-mail."

"I wish it were possible, too," the queen said. "I'll never forget you, Allie. I'll never forget any of you." And the queen gave each of them a hug—even Toby.

The four travelers got into the Volkswagen. Max pulled out a computer keyboard from between the seats. Allie, seated next to Max, opened the glove box. It was hard for her to see the power switch because her eyes were blurred with tears—but she found the switch and flipped it on.

Max tapped on the computer keypad, and some numbers came up on the dashboard display. Then Max pressed ENTER. The travelers waved good-bye—

And ten seconds later, Max, Allie, Grady, and Toby were in Max's backyard. It was the twenty-first century again.

They got out of the car and looked around. The party decorations were still up, the refreshment table was still piled with food—but there was nobody in the backyard.

"Where is everybody?" Grady asked. "Is the party over?"

"They're all in the front yard," Max said. "Toby, remember when you called for all those pizza deliveries, plumbers, and taxicabs to show up?"

Toby backed up a step. "Dude!" he said. "Don't blame me for that! You can't prove anything!"

"Easy, Toby, easy!" Max said with a grin. "It all turned out for the best. When I came back through the Doorway,

I found that everybody was in the front yard, looking at the biggest traffic jam this town has ever seen. They're out there now. So we've got a few minutes to put the lights, the fog machines, and the stereo back where I got them."

"You, too, Toby," Grady said. "You tried to wreck our party. The least you can do is help us put everything back where it belongs."

"No way," Toby said. "I've spent enough time with you dorks to last a lifetime!" And he dashed into the walnut grove, disappearing the same way he had arrived.

"Same old Toby," Allie said, shaking her head.

"Come on, guys," Max said. "Let's get everything set up!"

Max opened the hood and began unloading strobe lights and laser projectors.

"Max," Allie said, "don't you think you should tell your mom and dad where we've been?"

"Sure, I will," Max said. "Someday."

Flashback to 1945, a few months after the end of World War II.

A young American in uniform ambled down broad, busy Regent Street in London, just a short walk from Piccadilly Circus. For no reason in particular, the young American happened to notice a tiny shop with a modest little sign on the door that read:

Antiques and Relics

Gold and Silver

Objects of Vertu

Curious, he opened the door and walked in. Though the shop was dimly lit and narrow, it was crammed with interesting old things: paintings, chairs, tables, bookcases, chests, desks, clocks, porcelain, mirrors, rugs, candlestands, and in the center of it all, one golden Doorway. It was the Doorway that attracted the young American's attention.

"Interested in the Doorway, are you?" a voice said.

Startled, the young American turned. There was a shopkeeper behind the counter. Golden sunlight streamed in through the window of the shop—brilliant shafts of light that made it hard to see the shopkeeper's face.

"I like old things," the young man said. "I inherited a big old house back in the States, and I'm filling it with antiques."

"Ah," the shopkeeper said. "An American, eh? An airman, judging from your uniform. Stationed at Steeple Morden?"

"No. Alconbury."

"Well, you Yanks are all right with me. Welcome to Old Blighty. England, I mean."

"Thanks. What's the history of the old Doorway?"

"It was recovered from the ruins of Castle Mageste," the shopkeeper said. "The castle was hit by a stray rocket—one of the Nazi V2s. Horrible things, rockets. This Doorway was one of the few artifacts that survived the—"

Thump!

The shopkeeper was interrupted by a sound from the Doorway. The heavy door shook and swung open on its ancient hinges. A strange man leaped out of the Doorway and slammed the door behind him.

The stranger was tall, dressed like an ancient wizard, with a hooded cloak of deep satiny purple over long, flowing robes of velvety black. He looked at the American and stopped dead in his tracks. "*You!*" Doctor Delyrius shouted. "What are *you* doing here?"

"What do you mean?" the American said, backing away. "We've never met before!"

"You look older," Doctor Delyrius said, "but everything about you—you're McCrane, aren't you?"

The American looked shocked. "How did you know my name?"

"Max McCrane?"

"No, Horton McCrane."

"Wait—" The old man's eyes shifted. "What year is this?"

"Nineteen forty-five," Horton McCrane said.

"That's it! You're the boy's father—No! His *grand*-father!"

Horton McCrane took a step forward. "But I don't—"

"No!" Doctor Delyrius shouted. "Don't come near me! Stay back!" He dashed to the front door, flung it open, and ran outside.

"Hmph!" the shopkeeper said. "Bit of an eccentric."

"But where did he come from?" Horton McCrane asked. "I mean, was he hiding back there, or—"

"Well," the shopkeeper said, "you don't suppose he just popped in out of thin air, do you? Probably escaped from some asylum for the criminally disturbed. The bobbies will have him rounded up straightaway. Now, about this Doorway—"

"I'll buy it," the American said.

The shopkeeper blinked. "You Yanks are so impulsive!"

"I've got to have that Doorway!" Horton McCrane said. "I mean, look at what just happened! I walked into an antique shop and a strange man in a wizard costume jumped out of an antique Doorway and called me by name! When something that strange happens, there's got to be more to it than mere coincidence! There's something about this Doorway that deserves a closer look. Now, I want you to pack it up carefully and ship it to my home in America, Mister—what is your name?"

The shopkeeper smiled in the golden sunlight. "Call me Gavriyel."

TIMEBENDERS

BATTLE
BEFORE TIME

JIM DENNEY

Experience More
Time-Travel Adventures

in

BATTLE BEFORE TIME

Excerpt • Timebenders # 1 • *Battle Before Time*

"Max! Grady!" Allie whispered, standing on a rock beside the stream. "Look!"

The boys looked where Allie pointed. A white-tailed deer with a reddish brown coat was on the opposite side of the stream, next to a large boulder. As they watched, the deer bent its head to drink from the stream.

Splat! A big splotch of red and pink fruit exploded against the boulder. Some of it splashed on the deer. It looked startled and backed away from the fruit-splotch, blinking the juice from its large brown eyes. But it wasn't afraid.

Allie whirled and saw Toby up the hill, a nasty grin on his face. He held another piece of fruit in his hands and was preparing to throw again.

"Toby! No!" she yelled.

Toby hurled the fruit. It sailed in a high arc and landed in the stream, splashing water up on the stream bank—but it missed the deer by a good three feet. The deer looked at Toby with a curious expression, then turned, put its white tail in the air, and casually walked away.

Enraged, Grady scrambled up the hill toward Toby.

Smirking, Toby backed away toward the shade of the grove.

"Get out of here, Brubaker!" Grady yelled. "Just get lost!"

"No! Wait!" Allie called. "Toby, come down here with us! We don't know where the Enemy is or when he'll show up! We've got to stay together!"

"Dude!" Toby chuckled. "Like I want to hang out with a bunch of losers! I'm bored. I'm going to find something fun to do." He walked away, moving along the edge of the trees.

"Let him go," Grady said. "We're better off without him."

"You're wrong," Allie said. "I know Toby's been nothing but trouble, but we still need each other. I don't know what the Enemy intends to do to us, but I know we can't beat him if we're divided against each other."

Max trudged up the hill to join Grady and Allie. His shirt was soaked from his attempt to clean it—but the pink stains were still there. "Maybe I should go after Toby," Max offered.

"No," Grady said. "If the three of us get split-up, we're really sunk. Toby knows where to find us."

Allie glanced worriedly at the top of the hill as Toby

disappeared over the rise. "I just hope he comes back," she said, "before the Enemy shows up."

⊚ ⊚ ⊚

Toby trudged up the grassy hill in a foul mood. Occasionally, he saw a bird on a tree limb or a squirrel on the ground, and he would pick up a rock and try out his aim. Fortunately for the animals in Eden, Toby's aim wasn't very good.

"This whole trip is whack, man!" he grumbled out loud. "It's all McCrane's fault—him and his dorky Timebender! And Grady Stubblefield, the big man, always bossing people around! And Miss Holier-Than-Everybody Allie O'Dell! She's always like, 'Let's pray about it! Let's pray about it!' How lame is that? What is she, some kind of saint? And that Gavriyel, Mister Glow-in-the-Dark Tough Dude! Too big a coward to do his own dirty work, he has to send a bunch of kids to do it for him! That's totally messed up, man! That is so—*Oooof!*"

Toby tripped and went flying. For a few moments, he lay sprawled on Eden's grassy carpet. Then he clambered to his feet, using every swear word in his vocabulary. He looked down—

And saw a glint of silver in the grass!

He had tripped over something stretched across the ground, half-hidden by the tall grass. He bent down for a closer look, carefully parting the grass, and saw—

Something long, shiny, and mirror-polished. It seemed to be made of pure sterling silver, but intricately detailed, with perfectly formed scales, like the scales of a snake. Each scale was a shiny little mirror that reflected Toby's pudgy face in miniature. Whatever this silvery thing in the grass might be, it was shaped like a snake. It was long and curving, and it trailed through the grass and up the hill.

Toby followed the silver thing to see how long it was and where it led. And as he followed it, he found that it was encrusted here and there with glittering white diamonds, red rubies, green emeralds, and blue sapphires. It snaked around rocks and under bushes, leading right into a cave at the edge of a grassy clearing.

Reaching the cave, Toby parted the vines at the opening with his hands—and almost jumped out of his skin!

Toby stared into a huge reptilian face, like the face of a snake made of polished silver, with eyes of red fire. The pupils in the eyes were vertical slits of darkness, like the depths of a bottomless well. Twin curls of black smoke rose from its nostrils. A forked tongue flicked out between gleaming silvery fangs.

Toby Brubaker was face-to-face with the Dragon of Eden.